COLUMBUS AND THE FAT LADY

AND OTHER STORIES

COLUMBUS AND THE FAT LADY

AND OTHER STORIES

MATT COHEN

ANANSI TORONTO 1972

Cover design: Barry Rubin
Cover photo: Graeme Gibson

House of Anansi Press Ltd.,
Toronto, Canada

Printed in Canada by The Hunter Rose Company

ISBN: 088784-324-7 (paper); 088784-423-5 (cloth)
Library of Congress Card Number: 72-86027

1 2 3 4 5 6 7 8 79 78 77 76 75 74 73 72

Some of these stories have appeared in *Impulse* and on the CBC programme *Anthology*. TOO BAD GALAHAD first appeared in a limited edition published by Coach House Press.

The author wishes to thank the Canada Council and the Province of Ontario Arts Council for assistance during the writing of this book.

Other books by the same author

Korsoniloff
Johnny Crackle Sings
Too Bad Galahad

For Susan

CONTENTS

THE WATCHMAKER

The watchmaker's gold wallet is embroidered and stamped with a picture of the village green. Dense black hair sits on his head in uncombed clumps and there are small tufts from his nose that melt into his moustache. I see him standing outside of his shop, under the awning, his thick arms tapering down into delicate hands that have been shaped by small motions. At times I think he has no face. There is bone and flesh. There are networks of nerves, veins and arteries that lace through the surfaces. But sometimes he seems to have transformed himself into a blank, a man who sits in the corner and talks to the grandfather clock.

In his coat pocket there is a red satin cushion. This man plays the violin, has small hard calluses on the tips of the fingers of the left hand, is an unbeliever. It would be easy for him to do certain things. He could set all the clocks in his shop to different times. He could grow a beard. He could eat fish sandwiches for lunch or bet on horses. But he restrains himself. He fears that he will reduce his options, lose the mornings under the awning, earn the enmity of his grandfather clock.

His wife would like a new coat. His daughter would like to travel in Europe. He lives in the midst of expectations. So I see him in the summer, under the awning, standing in the shade not even pretending to look for customers. He is pretending he is a shopkeeper. Or he is just letting himself stand blankly for a moment. Perhaps he is unaware of what he looks like. But his wife and daughter must surely catch it sometimes, notice that he has disappeared.

In the winter I sit with him in the corner by the grandfather clock. I try to extract his wisdom, hoping he will dispense it in little lumps.

What is the time? I ask.

Two thirty, he replies. Then he turns to the grandfather clock and points at his huge pendulum. He laughs and drinks his tea. The clock is large and carved; its works shine like gold behind the glass. It ticks off the seconds. I feel that there are some seconds wasted, some in which I should have been doing something else. I fabricate my mortality. I ask him if he ever feels like that, if what he is doing is sitting by the grandfather clock letting his life escape.

Where to? he says. He turns off his face, he is resting his hand on the wooden side. Where to? he says, immensely pleased with his joke, as if it was some profundity he had eaten for breakfast.

Alright, I say conclusively, then you can invite me for supper.

It is a disaster. His daughter is unsure if I have been brought for her benefit. She refuses to play the piano. His wife, not knowing what to do, asks him to play the violin. It was unanticipated. He is not the kind of man you ask to play the violin. Still, he does it. He draws the bow out of the case first and meticulously brushes the horsehair with rosin. Then he takes out the violin and tunes it. When everything is ready he gets the cushion from his coat and tucks it under his chin. He stands in front of us, as if we are an audience that must be respected. I shall now play a certain sonata, he says. He nods his head and then begins to play.

Doesn't he play nicely? his wife says. It is as if there were a record on. When he is finished the watchmaker puts everything away and sits down. His wife finds this unremarkable.

He is about forty years old. He came to North America from Europe after the second world war. His accent has intonations of several languages, and when he speaks I feel that everything has been carefully considered in the light of everything. Any man who can survive being turned into a record must know something. What am I going to do? I ask him.

He laughs at me. It doesn't matter.

But, I say, you do something.

Then do something. He pulls out the stool with the chessboard. His hands wrap delicately around the pawns. I wonder if his wife notices it, this delicacy of his hands, or if he is only that way with inanimate things.

From seven to eight every morning I clean his shop. There is a small cupboard with all my appliances. I vacuum the floor, dust off the glass cases, polish the grandfather clock. Then I go home, just before he comes, and stand at the window. The clouds roll by like trains. I stand there invisibly watching the shop. Once a week I stay there until he arrives so he can pay me. In the afternoons I am a visitor, it is different.

Do you have a secret? I ask him point blank. If you don't have one how can you expect me to keep spending all this time here?

Then go, he says. He winks slyly at me and turns to the chessboard. I see, he says, that you will resign in seven moves.

One morning he didn't come to the shop. He was away for two days. Then he came back, sallow and drawn.

Were you sick?

I had a headache, he said. It was clear that there would be no discussion.

A few weeks later he was away again, this time for three days. I had a headache, he said. It was clear that there would be no discussion. But I persisted.

Alright, he said. I will tell you why I have the headaches. He leaned back in his chair, put his hand on the clock, and closed his eyes.

It was when I was a boy, he said. During the war. We lived in a town that no longer exists. There was my father, my mother and myself. They had seen the war coming, heard stories about what was happening, but when the news broke they were thrown into a panic. The house was in an uproar all the time. One day my mother would send me to school early, to get me out of the house. The next day she would make me stay home and hide in the attic. It went on that way for months. At any moment things would fly off in a different direction. Every day it was said there would be an invasion. Finally my father made up his mind. He told me to pack my things in a small suitcase. Then he took me on a journey. We travelled for two days on a train. We came to a town. You are going to stay with my brother, he said. He is the mayor. No harm will come to you.

But, I said, you never mentioned a brother.

Never mind, he said, I was saving it for a surprise.

He took me to the mayor's house. The mayor was a man much different from my father. He was remote and cold. He patted me on the head as if I was a baby. My father knew I didn't like him but he could do nothing. Everything is agreed, the mayor said. Then my father left.

A week later it happened: there were troops everywhere. In tanks, in jeeps, walking up and down the streets looking for someone to fight. They were billeted in the school and in people's homes. We had a captain at our house. He and the mayor would stay up half the night, drinking and discussing the war. People were always disappearing. There was one time when hostages were shot publicly. The mayor took me to see it. He put his hand on my head and forced me to look. I had no friends except the mayor's wife and there was nothing to do. One day her clock was broken and I fixed it. After that day I fixed clocks and watches. It seemed as if I had always known how. I even fixed the Germans' watches, though somehow I never got them quite right. There was an artillery officer who used to help me when necessary. Eventually the war changed and the Germans left. When the Americans came they didn't want their watches fixed. I asked the mayor when I would be going home.

Your parents are dead, he told me. They were killed two weeks after you came here. So.

And that is why you get the headaches?

No, he said. What I told you was what you expected to hear. If that was enough to give a man a headache the whole world would be in bed. He opened his eyes and patted the clock. The truth is, he said, that it isn't headaches at all. I wake up in the morning and tell my wife to leave the house. I am sick. Then I go back upstairs and lie down on my bed to think. He paused. Don't you want to know what I think about?

Yes, I said.

Good. He leaned back and patted the clock. I will tell you. What I think about is how it happened that my father, a man without a brother, left me at his brother's house. That is unusual, you must admit. It took me a long time to find out but this is what I discovered. . .

It is impossible to imagine what it was like to be young in Europe when my father was young. He came from a family of no wealth. He was a Jew. The old world seemed to be crumbling yet there was nothing, specifically, that he could have. It was after the first world war. He had been brought up very orthodox and was away from home for the first time. He was studying at a university. But what was he going to do after he studied? Was he going to be a professor? Impossible. A lawyer? How would a man like him, a man of no background, a Jew, get clients? He was a man without a future.

When you have no future the present becomes very important. He met a girl, the daughter of a Jewish merchant. He took her to concerts and had dinner at her house. They went for walks. He felt sorry for himself. He would never be able to afford to marry her. He had a sense that he must destroy something. Yet he was pulled in two directions. The girl was very attractive. She almost loved him. He almost loved her. Perhaps they did love each other. It would be impossible to know; there were other circumstances. They became very involved, going for their long walks in the afternoon. These were secret of course. A respectable girl did not do that in those days, not unless she was engaged. She began to see another man. A man who was older, who would be able to provide her with a house and a life. She felt little for the man but knew that it was inevitable.

My father discovered what was going on. He was young and hopelessly in love with himself, his great despair. The walks grew more frequent. He wrote her passionate letters and said he would kill himself. She was not unmoved by this. They would lie on the grass and my father would describe the various ways in which he might end his life. He would stab himself and shriek her name with his last breath. He would jump off a bridge reciting a poem in her praise. She found this disturbing. It aroused other instincts in her. As he described his suicide my father would caress her, perhaps even kiss her. She would return his kisses.

During this period the other man grew more persistent. He was an established man, a lawyer. He wanted to get married and have children. He couldn't wait forever. He pressed his suit and finally the girl agreed. My father, crushed, did not commit suicide: he left town. A few months later he heard that the man had married – but to a different woman. My father, by now securely in love with his beautiful memory, returned to see the girl. But when he got to the house and knocked on the door, no one answered. Finally he inspected the house. It was clear that no one had been there for months. Everything was out of trim. The curtains were closed.

Disappointed he went to a nearby café to make enquiries. He was told that something terrible had happened to the girl, that the whole family had left town. It was hinted that the girl was pregnant. All suspected that it was the other man. He found out where they were staying and went there. He knocked on the door. The girl's father answered and then, seeing who it was, slammed the door in his face. He knocked again. Go away, the old man shouted.

The next day my father came back. Every day, several times a day, he knocked on the door. Finally they let him in. The girl, of course, was pregnant. Everything was arranged and they got married.

And you were the child?

Yes, he said. I was the child. When the news of the war came my father didn't know what to do. He wanted to hide me somewhere but knew nowhere safe. Finally he hit upon the idea of appealing to the other man, the man who had been engaged to my mother, the man who was the mayor. At first my mother refused. But my father pointed out that there were no other possibilities. There was only one problem. How could he persuade the man to accept me?

He devised a plan. He knew that the other marriage had been barren and that the man had wanted a child. Perhaps he could convince him that he was my true father. It would be a flattering suggestion. Memory fades. My father was very pleased with his gambit. He explained it to my mother. She was curiously silent. It wasn't long before he had the whole story out of her: the man had refused to marry her when he found out she wasn't a virgin.

My father went to visit the mayor. He explained that he had discovered that the child was the mayor's. The danger was obvious. Would the mayor protect it? The mayor refused. What if someone found out he was harbouring a Jew? My father pressed his case. Look, he said, who could possibly know?

You could, the mayor said. If the child is not yours you might well want your revenge.

And so the bargain was made. The day the Germans arrived in my father's town they received a message that there were two members of a Jewish organization, at a certain address. When they searched the house they found guns and knives, the handwritten outline for a pamphlet. My father and mother were waiting in the living room.

And that is what you think about?

No. How can a man think about something like that? It would drive him crazy. He slapped his small hand against the side of the grandfather clock. The truth is that I stay home with my wife. I don't know what's gotten into her. She can't get enough.

His face had disappeared. There was bone and flesh: networks of nerves, veins and arteries laced through the surfaces. He was sitting still, watching the movement of the pendulum. Sometimes it took forever to go from one side to the other. Sometimes it moved so fast that it was almost invisible. Sometimes it stopped altogether.

He stood up. It was time to go home. He put on his coat with the red satin cushion in the pocket.

I see him standing outside the shop, under the awning. I go and visit him in the afternoons and we sit by the grandfather clock, drinking tea and playing chess. He says he has told me all his secrets; but still he tolerates me. I am patient.

THE END

THE END

Rombeck leaned back in his armchair. He had his feet wedged into the sides of the chair so that he could gaze, reflectively and contrapuntally, through his knees at his visitor.

Well James, Rombeck said. What brings you here today? In fact, he added, not without a trace of hostility, what brings you here any day?

James watched Rombeck's mouth, framed by his corduroy knees, as it enunciated the words. The truth was that James visited Rombeck for an easily understood but inexpressible reason. Rombeck served excellent espresso coffee and cheese sandwiches and James had no money and few friends.

Your excellent company Rombeck. Your virtuosity as a host and your incisive mind. You see, Rombeck, I have a problem. Only you can help me with it. Only you can say what needs to be said. Only you can understand it.

I see. Perhaps you are afflicted with Cupid's diseases and need some sort of medical sustenance.

No, Rombeck. Although as a doctor you are unsurpassed my physiology is adequate and not needing attention. No, Rombeck, it is my mind which is the cause of my suffering.

Come come James; look at you. You are a mess. Your skin is dull and lifeless. Your breath is rank. Your fingernails are bitten to the knuckle and your hair is falling out. In addition to suffering from vitamin deficiency and tooth decay you are probably in a pre-tubercular condition. Would you like me to arrange for an X-ray? Here, have a sandwich.

Thank you Rombeck. No Rombeck, though my hair and skin are dry and flaky and my eyes are bloodshot, and, I confess, my lungs are not all they could be, it is my mind that suffers. Tell me, Rombeck, what is the meaning of life?

Rombeck withdrew his hand from beneath the cushion of his easy chair. It concealed a small but useful derringer. From between his knees he sighted James's forehead and squeezed the trigger.

* * *

Professor Arnold Whizz was known and respected throughout the university community as a man and a scholar. Forty-five years old, he was at the peak of his powers. His first book, an amended version of his Ph.D. thesis, had established his reputation as a philosopher with an enquiring and original mind. His second book, *A Study In Chaos And Order*, had more than fulfilled the promise of the first. It was extraordinarily well-received by critics, one of whom called it "a magnificently lucid exposition of the tenets of rationality which transcends the ambiguity of experience to make a powerful and contemporary call for the return of the guidance of human affairs to Reason itself." It was known that his name was whispered in the highest offices and that, were he not committed to the direct exchange of the classroom, he would already be occupying one of those offices himself.

Professor Arnold Whizz's most popular course was the one he gave to third year Honours students. It was attended and audited by hundreds of students from all facets of the university community. The course was entitled *The Meaning Of Life*.

Because the course was so directly relevant to student concerns, Professor Whizz held numerous office hours during which students were free to consult him, individually, about the finer points of his lectures. His office, devoted as it was to the pursuit of knowledge, was appropriately appointed. A large Turkish divan lay atop a sumptuous rug. Erotic statues graced the walnut bookshelves. Professor Arnold Whizz was a degenerate.

His classes were primarily, though not exclusively, composed of females. In his office he spared no pains to assure that contact was made. Located beneath the couch was a switch that electronically controlled the lock on the door. Professor Arnold Whizz was not a man to shrink from reality.

On the other hand he was not indiscriminate. When James walked through the door with a Fearless Fosdick bullethole drawn in the centre of his forehead Professor

Whizz was prepared to do his duty although he certainly was not looking forward to it.

James sat down in the chair opposite Whizz's desk. Whizz pulled on his black silk gloves and smoothed them over his hands.

You know, James said, I have discovered the meaning of life.

And what, may I ask, is that?

James drew a derringer from his pocket and aimed it at Whizz's forehead.

Prepare to meet your end Whizz, he said.

Whizz leaned back in his chair and contemplated the void. Let me see that gun, he said. It looks like an antique.

Alright, James said. But be careful. It's loaded. He handed Professor Whizz the gun.

Whizz took the gun, aimed it at James's forehead and squeezed the trigger.

Hello Rombeck? Whizz here. I need a certificate.

Good man.

* * *

When James met his girlfriend Melissa that night he had two concentric circles in the centre of his forehead. The outer was black; the inner was red.

What's that James? Some new club? Do you have a magic marker with you?

No, Melissa. It is merely the mark of fate.

Look, James, I've got two tickets for the basketball game. Let's turn on and go watch the game.

For God's sake Melissa. Can't you see that I'm practically dead?

Well come on then. It'll cheer you up.

James leaned back in his chair and surveyed Melissa from across the arborite restaurant table. He took a bite from his toasted Danish and had a sip of coffee.

Melissa.

James?

Melissa have I ever described you to yourself?

No James.

Melissa. You are indeed a wonderful person. You have two kind and loving parents, three trusting and honest brothers, two beautiful sisters. Yet you are the jewel of the family for you know charity. James paused and took a bite of Melissa's clubhouse sandwich. Tell me, Melissa. What is the meaning of life?

Life James?

Yes Melissa, life.

Let me see. Oh yes. Life is the random diversification of chemical prototypes. In its higher forms it is endowed with consciousness and realizes itself by transforming order into chaos.

Order into chaos?

Oh. Sorry. Chaos into order. There. Did I get it right?

Perfect Melissa. Absolutely unblemished. Whizz would be proud of you. Tell me Melissa, what is the true meaning of life?

I just told you.

No, tell me what you think.

Well, let me see. Life is uh. Life is the, well, James, you know, chance of nature, a cruel trick is what it is. James, do you believe in God?

Maybe.

James. Melissa reached into her purse and pulled out a small but useful derringer. I'm sorry James. She aimed it.

Melissa. Let me see that derringer. I think it's an antique.

Alright. But be careful. It's loaded.

He took the derringer and pressed its muzzle to his forehead. He pulled the trigger.

Melissa got up and looked down at James's body sprawled on the floor.

Oh James, Melissa said. I never knew you really cared.

*   *   *

Rombeck leaned back in his armchair. He had his feet wedged into the sides of the chair so he could gaze, reflectively, and contrapuntally, through his knees at the visitors.

Well Whizz, Rombeck said. Have you composed it?

Whizz watched Rombeck's mouth, framed by his corduroy knees, as it enunciated the words.

Indeed Rombeck. Indeed I have. Whizz leaned back in his chair, surreptitiously dropping the cheese sandwich on the floor behind him. May I have the pleasure of reading it to you?

Of course Whizz. You know that is my desire.

Very well then, here it is.

We are gathered here today to pay our last witness to James Arlington Smith. A young man, filled with the promise of distinction, Smith died innocently and tragically at the hands of an uncomprehending society. Who killed James Arlington Smith? You and I killed James Arlington Smith. We are as guilty of his death as we would be if our hands were even now stained with his blood.

Come come Whizz. A little strong, *n'est-ce pas?*

Rombeck. Nothing is too strong in the face of reality. To continue.

What sort of man was James Arlington Smith? Let me tell a brief anecdote that will illuminate his character. One day, while in my office interviewing a student on the Socratic paradox, there was a knock at the door. Come in, I said. The door is always open. In walked James Arlington Smith. Although I had met the young man before, I had as yet only the most superficial knowledge of him. He had struck me, until that point, as a sickly young man, a person not entirely devoid of intelligence but one who was destined to be, at best, a superior sort of minor clerk.

Good day, he said, in that deadly serious tone which characterised his speech. Good day.

I liked the strong forthright look on his face. Here was a student who had no temerity in the face of knowledge. Humility yes but temerity no.

Sit down, I said.

He sat down in the chair opposite my desk. I'll not waste your time professor, he said. I'll come straight to the point.

How refreshing.

Indeed.

What is the meaning of life?

As you know, I am not one to shirk my responsibility as a teacher. Directly he had phrased the question and directly I would reply to it. I pulled out a derringer and aimed it carefully.

Wait, James said. I believe I know what you are going to say. Let me see that.

I handed him the derringer. Professor, he said. This is the true meaning of life. Then he put the muzzle to his forehead and pulled the trigger. I could not help, gazing at his body spread so finally on the floor, reflecting that there but for the grace of Reason, went I.

Melissa, all this time, was seated on the floor listening to the conversation of the learned men.

She looked at the window. James was standing outside on the fire escape, mouthing words at her. Open the window, he was saying, open the window. Melissa got up and opened the window.

Good evening gentlemen, James said. I trust the eulogy is proceeding apace.

Without a further word Rombeck and Whizz dropped dead on the spot. James and Melissa buried them in stale cheese sandwiches. Then, holding hands and with shining eyes, they left.

As they were walking down the street Melissa stopped and turned to James.

James?

Melissa?

Let's go to the basketball game.

Okay, James said. Why not?

OUR PASSION LIT THE NIGHT

Tollin had a strong sense of place in those years, walking up and down the treed streets of the Annex in Toronto, sitting on the steps of the tall baroque houses that had been subdivided into rooms or apartments, arbitrary dwellings that were visually separate from each other but whose sounds flowed in and out and back and forth so that finally he lived not in his own particular room but in a milieu of a certain predictable music, late-night footsteps and telephones ringing through walls. He moved from place to place almost casually, sometimes for no reason at all except to see what it would be like to look out of a window he had looked into, sometimes to erase a memory or change a mood. When he first lived there he felt like an anonymous stranger in a magic entertainment, but gradually as he moved about, was occasionally invited to parties or accompanied a girl who was babysitting somewhere, he got to know another side of the community, the more permanent residents who once, like him, had been enchanted with the area and now, prosperous, had settled with their children into a whole house, into an entire style of life which seemed to give them a special relationship to the treed streets and three-storey castles.

He had seen Barbara and David Kramer many times on the street, and although he had never met them he liked them already for the fact that they had not tried to modernize their house by painting it black and white or by putting huge picture windows into the brick walls. They were known as a relaxed and harmonious couple: the stability they exuded, their friendliness, and their easy and undemanding way of living made them popular. In the evenings there were often people at their house and in summer Tollin had noticed the sounds of music and warm laughter drifting out their open windows.

If there was a new movie, a play or a concert, it was inevitable that Barbara would telephone a few friends and ask them to come to the house afterwards. "Bring whoever you're with," she'd say. "David got some wood for the fireplace."

She was a slender and vivacious woman and beside David, who was big and heavyset with black hair and strong features, she looked almost childlike. Yet there was a docility about him, a gentleness that was not quite gentleness, that had the effect of making her complete devotion to him appear vaguely curious.

Several months after he first became aware of the Kramers, Tollin finally met them. He was in a bookstore, visiting a friend who worked there and browsing when Barbara came in. "Gail," Barbara exclaimed, she seemed so pleased to see her, "what a nice surprise. I was hoping you'd be here today. We're having a party tonight. You must come." She paused, noticing Tollin for the first time. "Aren't you going to introduce me?"

"Tollin Anderson," Gail said.

"How do you do," Barbara said. She was a few years older than Tollin, enthusiastically direct. "You *will* come tonight, won't you? Gail, make sure he comes." Barbara put her hands in her pockets. "Come over anytime, you know. You're always welcome."

When they arrived the house was already full of people. Tollin left Gail in the living room and went to the kitchen to get some wine. David and Barbara were there, standing at the counter rinsing glasses. "Come in," Barbara said. "The wine is right here. David, I want you to meet Tollin Anderson."

"Pleased to meet you," David said. He had a solemn way of speaking, as if he were afraid that his words might be misunderstood. Tollin was surprised at the softness of David's hand. It reminded him of a story about a mortician.

"Tell me about yourself," Barbara said. "What do you do?"

"Nothing much."

"How exciting. You should move to the country. Everyone is moving to the country these days."

David, finished with the glasses, excused himself and left the kitchen. Barbara walked over and stood beside Tollin.

"I've been dying to meet you," she said. "I've heard so much about you."

"I'm sure you say that to everyone," Tollin said.

"How did you know?" She was standing close to him. She rested her hand on his chest for a moment and then stepped back to the counter. She poured Tollin a glass of wine and lit a cigarette. "I'm sorry," she said. "I'm very tired this evening. Last night we were up late, John seemed to have a fever."

"John?"

"Our child."

"Of course," Tollin said. "The tricycle on the front steps. I almost tripped on it."

Barbara smiled and moved close to Tollin again. "He's usually very good," she said. "He almost never gets sick." She put her hand on his arm. "I hope you don't mind, if I ask how old are you?"

"How old do you think I am?"

"Twenty-three," Barbara said.

"That's right." Tollin was disappointed. He felt almost overwhelmed by her and moved away.

"Gail told me that you study music."

"I used to hide under the piano."

"I'd love to hear you play," Barbara said. "We're having some people over Friday night, would you – "

"No, I'm sorry."

"Don't be silly," Barbara laughed. "You don't have to perform for your supper."

People from the living room were searching out the wine in the kitchen. Tollin disengaged himself, deciding it was time to find Gail.

"Well?" Gail said, as he was walking her home, "How did you like her?"

"I don't know. I guess I didn't."

"You will. They're very friendly."

A couple of weeks later Tollin was walking down the

street past the Kramers' house and saw David sitting out on the steps. "Hello there," David called. "Beautiful day."

"Yes," Tollin said. He was standing at the end of the sidewalk. The leaves were beginning to turn.

"Come in and have a beer. I'm going to the West Coast," Kramer said, "to British Columbia. Doing a piece on young people living off the land." Kramer, in his mid-thirties, was a freelance journalist. Tollin had often seen his articles in newspapers and magazines. Tollin's beer had been served in a heavy pewter mug. On one side was emblazoned a university coat of arms. Below it, embossed in gold, was David's name. "I wanted Barbara to come with me and park John with my mother but she doesn't like to leave him, you know, for more than a night."

"I see," Tollin said.

"She likes you," David said. "Why don't you drop in sometime next week? Cheer her up."

Before he had decided whether to visit her Tollin happened to see her in the supermarket. While he was standing at the cash register she came up behind him and put her hand on his arm. "Hello there," she said. "How are you?" It irritated Tollin that she and her husband talked the same way. "Why don't you come over sometime, tonight maybe. You needn't worry about there being a party." She squeezed his arm slightly and then went back to her shopping.

Barbara answered the door in a red jumpsuit unzipped to reveal a diamond pendant and her collarbone. Her collarbone, homely and unintended, made Tollin feel suddenly less intimidated. They went into the living room. "This is Arnold," Barbara said. Arnold, wearing corduroys, a sweater and workboots, stood up awkwardly in front of the fireplace. He had a thick face, heavy eyebrows and an unconvincing moustache. "Arnold is a cartoonist," Barbara said. "He's come to live in Toronto." Barbara made tea and brought it in to them. She sat on the couch behind Arnold and stroked his hair while she talked. Arnold stared at Tollin the whole time. His workboots, his awkward manner, his bitten nails, all seemed essential to him, a visual explanation that accompanied him everywhere he went. While they drank their tea Barbara told Tollin about Arnold's portfolio of drawings, about the editor of a magazine who had said to David that he might give Arnold a job. When she had finished talking about Arnold she began complaining about her possessive mother-in-law. Finally she stopped. "Well," she said to Tollin, "tell us about yourself." She and Arnold looked at Tollin expectantly, as if he were about to deliver himself of his one and only life story. He noticed that they were holding hands. He wished he had some popcorn to give them. "Don't be shy."

"I'm sorry," Tollin said. He twisted his hands and looked down at his shoes. "You know how it is. When a person's spent a lot of time in jail they don't like to talk about themselves."

"Yes," Barbara nodded. Tollin kept his eyes on his feet and pushed the toes of his shoes together.

"Excuse me," Barbara said. "I'll get some more tea." She put on a record and then went into the kitchen with Arnold. There was a novel on the table beside him that Tollin had wanted to read. He put the novel in his pocket and left.

To support himself that winter Tollin gave occasional piano lessons and worked half days at the bookstore. The lessons were all on Saturdays so he was able to maintain a relaxed schedule. He had intended to practise seriously but found he was more interested in reading and sleeping. One morning, about ten o'clock, while he was sitting at his table drinking coffee, Barbara came to see him.

"I hope I'm not disturbing you." She hesitated at the door.

"No, come in."

"You're not busy?"

"No."

"Are you alone?"

"Yes," Tollin said. "Come in. I was just thinking of you.

I have that book of yours."

"Oh that," she said. She sat down at the table and took her cigarettes out of her purse. "Look," she said, "I hope I'm not intruding."

"No."

"You see," she said, "this is very awkward. I didn't think it would be."

"I'm sorry," Tollin said. "I should have returned the book."

"No. It's not that. Look. Did you know our child is adopted?"

"No."

"Well, it doesn't matter. Yes it does. You see, it seems that David is unable to have children." She accepted the coffee from Tollin and lit another cigarette. She looked away from him as she spoke. "Well, you see, I want another child and David has agreed that I could, you know, pick a person to be the father."

"That's very generous of him," Tollin said. "Does he get to pick the mother?"

"Very funny. You're making this difficult. You see, David and I agreed that you would be the person. Everyone says you're very intelligent and so, you see, you'd be an excellent father. Genetically speaking I mean. You weren't really in jail, were you?"

"Oh no," Tollin said. "I'm usually very good."

She reached across the table and put her hand on his. "You're very attractive," she said. "You're so young." Tollin sat and waited. Her palm felt like creased leather. Was she serious? He couldn't move. He was completely swamped in the physical sensations of nausea and desire. Barbara locked the door, closed the curtains, and sat down on Tollin's bed. "Come sit here," she said.

Tollin pushed himself up and started unbuttoning his shirt. "I have to be at work in two hours."

She left first. By the time he was outside, walking down the street, the event had receded, leaving only the knowledge that he had gone against himself and the question of why he had done it. "I don't know," he said to himself, kicking some brown November leaves along the sidewalk, "maybe I didn't know how else to get rid of her." The houses looked somehow different. He didn't see her again for almost two months.

She came by to say that she was pregnant and to invite him to dinner. "David wants to meet you again."

"Maybe he'll change his mind."

"He's very happy for me."

"For us?"

"Don't be silly."

Dinner was ravioli, salad and red wine. They ate by candlelight on a polished oak table. The reflection of the candles in the large round wineglasses, the spiced food, the crackling of the fire from the living room, the magnificent lustre of the oak surrounded them in an opulent womb. Perspiring, flushed with wine, David held up his glass and leaned forward. "To the baby," he said, looking directly at Tollin, "a toast to the baby."

"To the baby," Tollin said. He drained his glass.

"To the baby," Barbara echoed. She smiled. She noticed that David's plate was empty and passed him the ravioli. He helped himself and then handed it to Tollin.

"Eat," David said. "Eat." Tollin had an image of them pushing him to the floor and cramming ravioli into his mouth. He drank another glass of wine and played with his lettuce.

After dinner Barbara cleared away the dishes and said she was going upstairs to read John a story and tuck him in. David took a new bottle of wine and two clean glasses and led Tollin into the living room. "Well," he said. "You're almost part of the family now."

Tollin was too embarassed to reply.

"Now come on," David said, "there's nothing to be ashamed of. In fact I admire your courage. You're young — not that much younger than me but a different generation."

He had just published his feature article on West Coast hippies and was growing his hair. "You're too innocent," he said. "You have no idea how innocent you are."

"I don't know."

"Exactly. You can't know. You'll never know what it's like to learn, well, to *screw* in back seats and living rooms. Sex is so natural to you. But don't get me wrong," he patted his soft hands on his knees, "Barbara and I get along very well."

Tollin said nothing. He was beginning to suspect that the Kramers had evolved a plot to corrupt him. He consoled himself with the thought that he would not be seeing them again.

"Barbara is a beautiful woman," David said, without any trace of self-consciousness, "not just physically – she has a beautiful mind too. I couldn't leave her stranded, unconnected to the future."

Tollin felt that he was going to gag. He wanted to bring up all over the Kramers' beautiful expensive rug, their beautiful living room, David's stupid obtuseness, Barbara's bony chest, the robot-like child. He wanted to say something absolutely devastating, something that would shatter the composure of this complacent man, something that would get out everything he was feeling and leave him cleansed of the whole experience. But he couldn't think of anything at all. He felt dizzy. "Alright," he finally said, "you've had your little game. But from now on we play by my rules." As soon as he said it he felt absurdly adolescent. David refilled his glass from a bottle on the mantle.

"Touché," he said. "To the winner go the spoils. Seriously."

Barbara came into the room, kissed David on the top of the head, and sat down beside him. "Well then," she said, "you've settled it, have you?"

"Yes," Tollin said. "David and I will joust over your pale white flesh. In the end he will carry you off to a satin tent and you'll live happily ever after."

"Now don't be silly. You know we just wanted a baby." When she said that her face became hard and stubborn, as if she was determined that it was her version of reality that was going to be imprinted on the situation. David was smiling, docile and supportive.

"Alright," Tollin said. "You just wanted a baby. Well, thank you very much for the dinner and all." He went to the hall, put on his coat, and left. They saw him to the door, friendly and apparently without feeling that anything was wrong. When he looked back from the street they were silhouetted against the doorway, standing side by side looking out and waiting politely until he was out of sight.

Barbara came to visit Tollin one more time. It was in early February and she had to kick the snow from her boots at the door. "I'll take them off," she said.

"It doesn't matter." She took them off. Her feet showed veined and wrinkled through her nylon stockings. She sat down at the table while Tollin made some coffee.

"Don't you find me attractive?" she was saying.

"No."

"Yes you do."

"So what?" Tollin said.

"You know."

"I thought you were already pregnant."

"I am," Barbara said.

"Well then, forget it."

"Look," she said, "there's something I have to tell you. David is going to leave me."

"I wonder why?"

Barbara burst into tears. Tollin found her ugly when she was crying. It released her hold on him. He wondered if she used glycerine. "Hey," he said, "I've got an idea."

Barbara tried to look like a child smiling through her tears. "What?"

"Why don't you have an abortion?"

After a while Barbara lit a cigarette and stopped crying.

"David said that if he felt, well, *comfortable* with you he wouldn't leave."

"Look," Tollin said, "David isn't going to leave you. He needs you and you need him. You're very happy together. He was just saying that because he's feeling resentful. Why don't you go home and make it up with him?"

"On one condition."

"No."

"You come to dinner every week so David, you know, feels better about things."

"I'd feel better about things if we just forgot this whole game."

"Don't be silly. It's not a game. *Please.*"

"I'm sorry," Tollin said. "Here, sign this." He took a piece of paper and wrote out a few sentences saying that he was in no way responsible for the conception or care of any child born to Barbara Kramer. She signed and dated it. Tollin made her show him her driver's licence to check the signature. "Now," he said, "I'm going to put this in a safety deposit box, so don't bother searching through my room for it if you change your mind. Give me five dollars for the first year's rent." She pulled out her wallet; it was bulging with money. She laid two twenties on the table between them. Tollin took one of her matches and lit it. He burned the first twenty dollar bill in the ashtray. Then he took a five out of her wallet and put back the second twenty. For the first time in weeks he felt completely relaxed. "Now, tell me what this is all about."

"I told you," she said. "We wanted a baby. I always wanted to be pregnant, to know what it was like. It was David's idea. He suggested artificial insemination. But it seemed too cold and mechanical. I wanted something more human."

"Our passion lit the night," Tollin said.

"It was in the morning."

He stood up and went to the window. "I thought I'd never get over you," he said. "For days I lay under my bed weeping and singing Indian Love Song. I thought it would never end."

"It doesn't have to," Barbara said.

"Then I locked myself in my cupboard. I was going to hang myself from the lightbulb. There was a roll of drums and the band started to play. I decided to join the Foreign Legion instead."

"Stop it."

"I was inconsolable. Wild with grief. You were the first person I ever met who seemed to care, truly care, about me as a human being. You were so honest with me. I never doubted you for a moment."

"I *was* honest with you."

"Oh yes," Tollin said. "You were. You bared everything to me. Even the sweet pain of having to take a stranger into your faithful arms."

"It wasn't that bad."

"Oh no," Tollin said. "It was wonderful." He was still standing at the window. He clapped his hands. "I've got it. Let's take off your clothes and I'll whip you with the old school tie."

Barbara lit a cigarette and looked away from him. "Oh shut up Tollin, you're too young for that sort of talk."

"I'm sorry," Tollin said. "I forgot my place." He sat down again. "What ever happened to Arnold?"

"Who?"

"Arnold, the boy-wonder cartoonist."

"Oh," she said. "Arnold. He wouldn't do it. He said it was immoral. He wanted me to go away with him. He couldn't understand, not like you."

"You know why I did it? To get rid of you."

"Don't be silly," Barbara said. "You did it because you wanted a baby. You wanted to know that somewhere in the world there would be someone with your blood. I bet you hope it's a boy." She smiled at Tollin. He noticed that she had a very wide mouth. "The trouble with you," she said, "is that you don't know yourself very well. You should see a psychiatrist."

"Me? You're the one who's crazy. You're right out of your mind. You, your husband, and that stuffed toy you read stories to every night. You should all be locked up."

"No," Barbara said gently, "I'm not crazy at all. I'm in complete control of everything." She put her cigarettes in her purse and stood up. "We'll expect you Sunday."

After that Tollin went to the Kramers for dinner every second Sunday. He would arrive at six and leave at nine. They would eat their food, chat casually for a while, and then Tollin would help with the dishes. Without anything being said it had been agreed that after the baby was born Tollin would cease to see the Kramers. One afternoon, when he was at the bookstore, there was a phone call for him. "It's a boy," David was shouting over the phone, "come down to the hospital as soon as you can." David met him at the door to Barbara's room. "Come and see the baby," he said. They walked down the corridor to the room where the babies were kept, behind a plate glass window. "There it is," David said. "Second row, fourth from the end."

"Congratulations, David," Tollin said. He tried to sound as if he was saying what he was saying. He extended his hand to David. "Congratulations, old man."

"Thank you," David said.

"Aren't you going to give me a cigar?"

"Oh Jesus, I almost forgot." David reached into his inside coat pocket and pulled out a cigar. "Here," he said, "it's Cuban, the real thing. Now come and see Barbara."

Barbara was lying in bed, awake. She seemed exhausted but happy. There was a dozen yellow roses and a camera on her night table. "David says he looks just like me," she said. "Don't you think so too?"

"Absolutely," Tollin said.

Shortly after the baby was born Tollin moved to Montreal. Four years later he moved back to Toronto and, though many things had changed with him, he thought it would be nice to re-introduce himself to Toronto by working at the old bookstore again. He looked up from his invoice slips one day to see Barbara coming into the store, accompanied by the child. He recognized them immediately. Barbara was as slender and vivacious as ever. The child looked exactly like David. He was big for his age, he had the same round brown eyes and there was a characteristic docility in the way he moved.

Barbara didn't seem at all surprised to see him. "Hello there," she said. She stood beside Tollin and put her hand on his arm. "Meet David Junior. Doesn't he look nice? He's all dressed up."

THE NURSE FROM OUTER SPACE

Too many people, including you and me, sit around wondering whether we really come from outer space. Of course we come from outer space. It's time to stop wondering about it and start putting it all together. I have a friend called Arthur. Everyone has a friend called Arthur. It is a very common name. Arthur lives in a room in an empty house. He wakes up every morning at seven o'clock sharp. That is the way of the world.

One morning, when Arthur woke up, it was raining. He could hear the sound of rain dripping off the roof of his empty house. And, laid neatly on top of the sound of water, he could hear the spikey tapping of high heels. He sat up in his bed and looked out the window. A woman with an umbrella was walking in front of his house. She stopped at the corner, took a chocolate bar from her raincoat pocket, and ate it. When she was finished she threw the wrapper on Arthur's lawn and crossed the street.

The sound of her high heels faded off into the distance and Arthur lay down again on his bed. He listened to the rivers of water running from his roof onto the ground. Then he got out of bed and went down to the kitchen.

Like everyone from outer space Arthur is a terribly lazy person. He seldom works, his laundry is unspeakable, and most of the time he forgets to wind his watch. Although he has always known he was from outer space – his mother told him – Arthur has never really gotten hold of the fact. He could have made a career of it and dressed up in strange clothes and interviewed people. Or he could have gone into electronics and spent his evenings constructing a radar set. Instead Arthur evolved an entirely original hobby. He moves into empty houses and makes plans for interior decoration. Unfortunately he has no sense of colour or proportion so his plans are completely uninteresting.

Jack Kerouac once wrote that you should open up your mind and let it all happen spontaneously: the muse takes care of her children. Arthur follows his advice. Talking to him is like taking a shower. Writing about him is like trying to compose the yellow pages from memory.

Down in the kitchen Arthur did what he always does in the morning. He drank orange juice, ate two pieces of toast, and had a cup of coffee. Then he went upstairs and put on his clothes. It was exactly seven thirty-three. Arthur, dressed and fed, went outside to pick the candy wrapper off his lawn. He put it in his pocket, brought it inside, and made another cup of coffee. Then he sat at the kitchen table and stared at the wall.

There are many reasons why people from outer space may have been placed on this earth. One possibility is that at some time in the future an alien ship is going to land and take over the earth. During the Christmas holidays I met an ex-priest who holds this view. He is from Newfoundland. His theory is that pollution and war and misery don't matter because everyone enjoys them and one day strange creatures will come from outer space and set things right. We are here to welcome them. When they arrive a switch will be thrown and we will all go into action. In the meantime we live awkward uncoordinated lives and appear to be parasites on the mundane world. That is all part of it.

But Arthur was not staring at the wall waiting for the invisible switch to be thrown. The reason he is here on this earth is to do things that other Earthlings can't do. For example Arthur fills up empty houses. He moves into them and makes all sorts of plans. The fact that the plans are terrible makes no difference: they represent love and it is Arthur's special knowledge that empty spaces need love. That is why they are empty.

It would be nice to write a sentimental story about Arthur's love of empty spaces. One could compose a sweet vignette about Arthur sitting on the edge of Lake Ontario filling the sky with love. Or Arthur in a subway. Or Arthur in a cigar store. But that is not the story that has to be written about Arthur; that is a nurse story and the only time I tried to write a nurse story I got stuck on the sex scene. How do nurses make love? Of course they make love like everyone else but there must be some special imagery, some unique consciousness, some set of esoteric techniques that distinguish the way nurses make love. I am ashamed to admit it but I have never made love to a nurse. Neither had Arthur. He had never even met a nurse.

This is all getting very chatty. Chatty is something writing is not supposed to be. Good writing is tense, taut, evocative. Words bounce off each other like fleeing gazelles. My wife, who is not a chatty person, has the unfortunate quality of being a good listener. She says that while people are busily chattering away they send off little invisible cues which tell you how they want you to be. If you don't catch all those little cues then you are from outer space. If you do catch those cues you probably wish that you didn't.

Arthur is so oblivious to the cues that even if you told him they were happening he wouldn't believe it. He would think that you were harassing him. Arthur always thinks that people are harassing him. He is always wrong. It is so absolutely obvious that Arthur is Arthur that it is pointless to try and get him to do anything. Even if you are a nurse.

Arthur yawned and rubbed his eyes. It seemed to him that he was waking up a little earlier every day. That is one of the benefits of being a man of property. He shifted in his chair; his movement made him aware of the wadded candy wrapper in his pocket. He took it out and spread it in front of him on the table. He read over the list of ingredients and noticed that most of them were chemical. Then he turned the wrapper over: in regular neat handwriting was a name and telephone number. Katherine Smith, R.N., 756-5123.

Another theory about outer space is that there are already many developed races who live on planets far from Earth. They have arranged an inter-galactic treaty which has as its basis a police force of robots. Any time someone commits aggression against someone else, a robot sees it and eliminates the aggressor. Arthur and I had watched a movie with the same plot on my television set. The point that the man from outer space was making, the point that the Earthmen were only barely able to comprehend, was that the Earth had now developed its technology to the point where it would soon be a menace to other planets. It is a scientific fact that if there were a city as big as New York on the surface of Mars, we would be able to see it from Earth.

Arthur got up from his chair and walked into the living room. The living room was absolutely empty. It had a bay window so it was even emptier than it might have been otherwise. He sat on the ledge of the bay window and looked out at the street. He tried to remember what the woman had looked like but could only recall the sound of her high heels counterpointing the rain. Considering that she was a prostitute, her handwriting was very neat. He had always thought that prostitutes were illiterate. But she was a nurse too. What kind of nurse would leave her name and telephone number where absolutely anyone could find it?

There was one significant clue. She had stopped and waited a few moments before crossing the street. Perhaps she had left it specifically for him. It wasn't impossible. She might live nearby and have seen him coming and going. Maybe she had even intended to knock on the door but had lost courage and left the wrapper instead. After all it was a quiet neighbourhood.

The most important rule to keep in mind when writing a short story is that every word must count. Every short story writer and every short story reader knows that rule and Arthur was no exception. He walked back into the kitchen to examine Katherine Smith's short story. It contained a name, a telephone number and the letters R.N. Her story was so economical that she had only needed two words, an abbreviation and a number to tell Arthur everything necessary. To demonstrate that she knew what she was doing she had written her whole story on the back of a candy wrapper and thus had not wasted even one piece of paper.

When Arthur got to the phone booth he didn't hesitate. He walked inside, spread out the wrapper, and put in his dime. The woman answered on the second ring. She sounded very cool and self-possessed. "Hello," Arthur said. "Someone left a chocolate bar wrapper with your name and telephone number written on it on my front lawn. I thought you should know."

"I do know," the woman said. "I left it there myself."

"There is one thing you should be told."

"Tell me."

"It's too good to publish." He hung up and went out of the phone booth. It was eight-thirty in the morning. People were lined up at the bus stop waiting to go to work. People were walking up and down the street looking for an open store. Some of them carried empty shopping bags.

Arthur walked the two blocks back from the telephone booth and then he went upstairs to brush his teeth. When he had finished brushing his teeth he decided to go downstairs again and finish his plans for the living room. It was a large room with a bay window which made it slightly emptier than it would have been otherwise. He wanted to line the walls with bookshelves and put a big gold and red rug in the middle of the floor. When he was half way down the stairs the doorbell rang. His visitor was a woman, the woman whom he had seen that morning, Katherine Smith, R.N. and short story writer. She looked about thirty-five, had faded blond hair and, Arthur thought, rather British features.

"Good morning. My name is Katherine Smith. May I come in?"

"Of course." Arthur led her through the empty dining room to the kitchen. "Would you like some coffee?"

"Thank you." The woman was wearing a light-coloured raincoat, the same one she had been wearing before, and was carrying a purse. She hung the raincoat on the back of her chair and took some cigarettes from her purse.

Arthur didn't smoke but he had an ashtray. He put the ashtray on the kitchen table. Katherine Smith lit a cigarette, inhaled deeply, and set it in the ashtray. Arthur noticed that there were lipstick marks on the filter. He filled the kettle and turned on the stove.

People from outer space recognize each other but they seldom mention the subject until they are close friends. It sounds incredible but it's really no different from sex.

"Do you do a lot of revisions?" Arthur asked.

"Yes. Sometimes twenty or thirty. I'm getting sick of chocolate bars."

"How do you know which words to use?"

"They come to me in the night."

"What exactly is your *genre*?"

"Classified advertisements. Especially personals. Arthur call Katherine. All is forgiven."

"Katherine, meet me at my house at nine o'clock, Arthur."

"Arthur: the kettle boils."

"I would have said the pot boils."

"That is the difference between a professional and an amateur. The difference between the vernacular and literature. In a word, the difference."

"What word?"

Katherine got up and made the coffee. She brought milk from the refrigerator and pulled two packages of sugar from the top drawer.

"Do you sleep well?" she asked.

"Oh yes," Arthur said. "I always fall asleep very quickly. But I'm quite awake now. Would you like another cup of coffee?"

"I haven't finished this one yet."

Arthur sat at his kitchen table, drinking his coffee and dissembling. In the early morning it had rained – he had heard rivers of water running from the roof to the ground. Now the sun was out. He imagined the ponds of water on the road and sidewalk.

The story proceeds in fits and starts. The gradual development of character, the unfolding of the action, the creation of a private cosmology all take place within a few pages. That is why all the true masters of the short story live in attics.

"Do you sleep well?" she asked.

"No," Arthur said. "I wake up earlier every morning."

She looked at him closely. If his origins had not been obvious to her she would have thought him a desperate man. She would have thought that he had been so scarred by the world that he had put on a mask of false craziness to hide himself, to eliminate the necessity of responding to anything. She would have thought him vacant and ruined. She would have taken him by the hand and led him gently up the stairs and laid him like a baby on his single bed. Half absent-mindedly, looking out the window at the corner where she had stood and eaten her chocolate bar, she would have undressed him and made love to him at ten o'clock in the morning.

Another day they would have walked to the lake. They would have watched the seagulls in the lonely sky and filled its emptiness with their love. They would have eaten sandwiches and oranges by the lake and filled the afternoon with silence.

"Would you like to see my house?"

"Yes," Katherine said.

He took her by the hand and led her to the living room where the bay window billowed out towards the street. He led her up the stairs and laid her gently on the bed. Absent-mindedly, looking out the window to the corner where she had stood in the morning rain composing her perfect story, he undressed her. Then he took off his own clothes and lay down, precariously, beside her on the single bed. In the ten o'clock morning stillness he made love to her. She closed her eyes and saw the streaks where the rain had dried on his window. In the afternoon he took her to the museum and they walked around its old emptiness, filling it with the sharp sounds of her high heels and the quiet rhythms of their breathing. The next sunny day they went down to the lake. They saw a heron, older and balder than it should have been, hopping about the shore and striking poses for them in the warm breeze.

"Yes," she said, "that's the difference between a professional and an amateur." She was sitting with Arthur in his kitchen eating a piece of toast. They had spent the evening writing a novel.

Wanted: old candy bar wrappers.
free pick-up and delivery.

"Why do you say delivery?" Arthur said.

"It goes with pick-up. People would feel uncomfortable if it was left out."

Arthur snuggled his feet into his slippers and sipped his hot chocolate. Making love to a nurse wasn't much different from making love to an ordinary woman. She reminded him, though only distantly, of a telephone operator he had once known.

Every morning, all year round, Katherine would wake up at six o'clock. She would get dressed and walk to an all-night restaurant. She would sit there and drink a cup of coffee and write her short story on a candy wrapper. Then she would re-wrap the chocolate bar and walk back to the house. By the time she got there it would be about seven o'clock. She would stand on the corner for a few moments to make sure that Arthur was awake. Then she would drop the wrapper on the front lawn and walk around the block. There was a place, a small opening in a hedge, where she could sit privately and watch for Arthur. After an hour, sometimes two, he would leave the house and go to a telephone booth. When she saw him leave she would walk in the opposite direction to her own telephone booth.

"Hello," he would say, "someone left a chocolate bar wrapper with your name and telephone number written on it on my front lawn. I thought you should know."

"I do know," she would reply. "I left it there myself."

There is one thing you should be told," he would say.

"Tell me."

"It's too good to publish." He hung up and went out of the phone booth. It was eight-thirty in the morning. People were lined up at the bus stop waiting to go to work. People were walking up and down the street looking for an open store. Some of them carried empty shopping bags.

Arthur walked the two blocks from the phone booth to his house. He went upstairs to brush his teeth. When he had finished he decided to go downstairs again and complete his plans for the living room. It was a large room with a bay window which made it slightly emptier than it otherwise would have been. When he was half way down the stairs the doorbell rang. His visitor was a woman, the woman he had seen that morning, Katherine Smith, R.N. and short story writer.

"Good morning. My name is Katherine Smith. May I come in?"

"Of course." Arthur led her through the empty dining room to the kitchen. "Would you like some coffee?"

"Thank you." Katherine was wearing a bright summer dress, the same one she had been wearing before, and was carrying a purse. She took a package of cigarettes out of the purse.

Arthur didn't smoke but he had an ashtray. He put the ashtray on the kitchen table. Katherine lit a cigarette, inhaled deeply, and set it on the ashtray. Arthur noticed that there were lipstick marks on the filter. He filled the kettle and put it on the stove.

When the kettle was boiling Katherine got up and made the coffee. She had some sugar with her, sugar that she had taken from the restaurant.

"How do you do it like this?" he said. "How can you be so consistent?"

"I don't know," she said. "I guess that's the difference between a professional and an amateur."

"Tell me the secret of your short stories."

She stirred her coffee. "An editor once told me that the secret of a short story is to have a good ending."

"Would you like to see my house?"

"Of course."

He took her by the hand and led her to the living room where the bay window billowed out towards the street. He laid her down, gently on the red and golden rug. He closed the curtains so that the ten o'clock morning light came softly through to them. Absent-mindedly, precariously, he undressed her in the curtained morning and filled her emptiness with love. Absent-mindedly, precariously, she undressed him in the curtained morning and filled his emptiness with love.

KEEPING FIT

When he had started training it was always the breath that went first. That didn't surprise him; he knew that at thirty-two and with ten years of inactivity behind him it would take a long time. But after a couple of weeks, when he had worked up to doing a slow mile and had quit smoking, it became his legs and ankles. It wasn't for several months, when he was running six and seven miles at a stretch, that his feet began to bother him. It was funny; he had never thought of himself as having particularly good feet but somehow he had never encountered the problem of blisters and sores. But by the time he was up to ten miles the pain was always and exclusively in his feet. No matter what he did – he had tried all sorts of salves – even an antibiotic a couple of times – there didn't seem to be any way he could prevent the blistering. He remembered the difficulty of getting into condition too well to stop running for a couple of weeks to let his feet heal so he just bandaged them up and did his best to ignore them. If he was running smoothly, and lately he was always running smoothly, it took at least six miles for the bandages to work themselves off. After the first irritation of squashing them to a more comfortable place in his shoes it was two or three miles until they really started to hurt. He would run another fifteen minutes thinking of almost nothing but his feet and feeling the separateness of each sharp pain. Finally the hurt would melt together and he would run until he had to stop. The bandages were coming off now, he had felt the first twitch at the bottom of the hill; once they started they worked loose pretty fast. He ran easily along the shoulder of the level stretch of highway. The cars didn't bother him and he had long ago quit caring about people staring at him. Actually, he liked running along level ground even better than downhill and had, for a while, considered moving west. There was a feeling of continuous motion that, after the first few minutes, he would slowly sink into. When he had first been able to do ten miles he had thought about giving up his project and becoming a long-distance runner. He went out one night to a track club; it was summer and they practised in the evening. But, not really to his surprise, he found running with other people distracting. So he never went back and instead kept running on the streets and by the highway. He was half way at least through the painful part now. It didn't seem as bad today though he wasn't sure whether he liked that or not. As usual he couldn't think very clearly when he ran. In fact he could hardly think at all. That was one of the things that had attracted him to it. He thought a lot afterwards, about what he was doing and about other things. But when he ran he thought of nothing and was only barely conscious of his own movements and, of course, the cycle of his foot blisters. Going around a bend of the highway there was a last brief moment of sharp pain and then it all diffused. He loped along for another couple of hundred yards and turned onto a dirt road. It extended at least ten miles, according to the map, and he knew that would be far enough. He kept running. The motion had taken him over. After a while, he didn't know how long, he noticed he was slowing down and speeded up a little before settling into his customary rhythm. He had wanted it to be like that, smooth and easy, an imperceptible transition, and when they found him the next day they thought he had collapsed in mid-stride.

COUNTRY MUSIC

COUNTRY MUSIC

There was an old lady who lived near a dump. The old lady got tired of looking out her window at the dump so she spent two whole summers cleaning it up and planting flowers on top. I was driving down the road one day and where there used to be a dump I saw a garden. I got out and went over to look at it. There were plastic flowers and from close up you could see the edges of dusted tin cans growing out of the soil.

The old lady waved at me from her window so I went in and had a cup of tea with her. Yes, the old lady said, I guess those Frank brothers are pretty crazy. They take after their father, Old John MacRae. He was even crazier but he only showed it once or twice. Once was right after the war, he had come back to live with us on the family farm even though he wasn't wanted. One day he got so mad he ate a half a sack of potatoes. Wasn't sick either. Best appetite and biggest belly in the history of the township. He said he would finish the sack but he wanted to leave himself something for dinner. Then he walked out of the house and wasn't seen for a week. He was my own brother too. I don't even know if I wanted him to come back. He did though. Came back and finished off the potatoes.

Patrick Frank used to drive his old Ford truck into town every Wednesday afternoon to buy groceries and hang around the hardware store. He liked to shoot a game of pool there but they closed the hall after Joe Canning tried to set fire to the owner. He walked in with a can of kerosene, poured it over Mr. Liston, and lit it. Now Mr. Liston builds cottages for tourists and owns the drugstore. Joe Canning is in jail for setting fire to a barn. Patrick Frank is parked in a field forever. He wanted to buy one of the tables after the pool hall closed but they were sold, all at once, to someone from Toronto.

Patrick Frank's twin brother Mark is known to be the crazier of the two. Once he got so drunk lying in the hot summer sun that he passed out on the side of the road. Pat Frank and Billy Clenning saw him there so they went and got a can of black rustproofing paint, some deluxe off-white wall enamel that was in the barn and an old roll of wallpaper and took off all his clothes and decorated him. Mark Frank was so drunk that when he woke up he didn't even realize what had happened until he tried to pull down his wallpaper to have a crap. But that wasn't the incident that made everyone think he was crazy.

Driving out from town, along the road that goes to town, you come to a place where there are a whole bunch of little roads going out from the main road. The little roads lead to cottages and farms. At the place where the big road starts turning into little roads is a general store. Since the turn of the century the store has been burned five times and gone through a dozen owners but right now it is a lucrative business in the summer. People around here are terrible liars, one woman told me. When Mark Frank found he had been decorated he was so happy that he went to the store to show it off to everyone. A retired engineer and his wife from Florida were buying baked beans and maple syrup when in walked Mark Frank wearing nothing but paint and a strip of wallpaper down his backside.

Howdy folks, said Mark. One false move and I'll shoot you dead.

You meet some crazy people where you least expect them and sometimes it makes you wonder how they got that way. And of all the crazy people in the county it was agreed that Pat and Mark Frank were the craziest. Welfare drunks, that's what they were, welfare drunks. Pat Frank was tall and fleshless as a desert runner. He played fiddle at all the parties for thirty years. Held it against his chest and made up songs to go with it.

I was leaning against an old half ton truck, watching Mark Frank cut through another half ton truck with a welding torch. There wasn't just one half ton truck, or two, there were more than I could count. Saved them for tires, he said, for tires and trailers like the one he was making me by cutting off the box of a truck that hadn't moved for twenty years. He was sober all that summer, so he said, at least while his brother was in the hospital. Used to play the fiddle like no one you ever heard, always had a smart answer for anything you might say. When he picked him up off the floor to take him to the car you couldn't believe how light he was. The man had disappeared from drinking.

People out here are terrible liars. That's what one woman told me. We were sitting on her front porch and she was telling me lies. Now she's married to a prosperous farmer but once she was known to be going out with Mark Frank. After he turned into his true self, which anyone could have predicted, she used to get teased about how she almost married him. I can see you now, her husband would say, you'd be drinking and singing away just like the rest of them. I bet you wish you married him instead of me.

And everytime he says that she blushes and says well who was that floozy you used to take to the movies. I guess you only needed one when she gave you what you wanted.

And everytime she says that he just grins and slaps the table. Now you know that isn't true, he says. I never bothered taking her to the movies.

People out here are terrible liars, the woman said to me. You can't trust a thing they say. Now that old lady, the one up the road, she's an aunt to the Frank twins and she told them that their father would have married the widow Frank if he hadn't been crazy. Why he only went and saw her because he was in a state of shock. It was his unconscious mind that made him do it. When he realized what he had done he got out of there so fast you couldn't have believed it.

What's this unconscious mind stuff?

It's what a person has in his head that he doesn't know. Like the way a cow always goes for a garden.

When Pat Frank got out of the hospital he would have killed himself if he hadn't passed out first. A man can't drink too much when he's been in bed for two months. You have to get used to it. Mark Frank and I were passing a wine bottle back and forth in his junkyard. Now people like you, he said, you come out to the country but you see things through city eyes.

I don't know, I said, right now I can hardly see a thing.

That's right, he said. Only good thing to be said for you is that you know it.

I bought the wine, I said.

But the bottle's empty. He threw it through the windshield of an old Chevrolet that had been waiting for it these past fifteen years. Never mind, he said. He reached into his shirt and pulled out a mickey. Now you look over at that house there and what do you see?

What house? All I could see was a bump in the field.

That's my mother's house, he said. Stood there for fifty years without moving. Burned down two winters ago. Only problem is, he said, hogging the bottle, you can't live in it now.

Tell me about your Aunt, I said.

The old lady?

Yeah.

I don't know, he said, there isn't anything to tell. Only see her once a year at Christmas. If the snow's not too bad.

What does she do all day?

I don't know, he said. Listens to the telephone. Can't make a phone call without her breathing down your neck. I tell her to get off the line but it doesn't do any good.

The old lady who lived by the dump had been married to a man named Tom Gorman. No one remembered anything at all about him except two things. The first gets told about three times a month: one time when a shed was burning he picked up a two hundred pound pig under each arm and carried them to the house. The remarkable thing about this was that the man was lame. The second thing, which people have forgotten about, is that he hated John MacRae, his wife's own brother, one-time lover of the widow Frank and father of the craziest twins in the county. And because the old lady is the widow of the man who hated their father the twins only visit her once a year and not even that if the snow's deep.

This and more Billy Clenning, comrade-in-arms of the Frank brothers, told me as we sat by the lake sampling his home-made wine. Right from where we sat we could see the old sugar house that John MacRae had built, the only thing he ever did in his life except spend a night with the widow Frank.

Billy Clenning's father and lame Tom Gorman had been pretty good friends. Especially good friends in a place where people never get too close. To celebrate their friendship and the spring every year they boiled down some maple syrup. They would sit and drink and keep the fire going for a couple of weeks. It made them enough syrup and sugar to carry them through the year and sell a bit besides.

There are places you can walk, pockets and valleys, where you can't see any signs of the last fifty years: no hydro poles or metal fences, not even roads except for old ruts that might have been gouged by a wagon. So that's what it was like when John MacRae decided, after ten years in the war and in the city – from here the two are almost the same – to make his return to the old homestead. In that ten years he had never sent any communication at all. He showed up, in his fashion, one Sunday at church – dressed up in city clothes and sporting a moustache. There is a picture of him in his fancy clothes and moustache in the old lady's kitchen. She pointed it out to me one day when we were playing cards. He is sitting on top of an old pine hutch in a gilded frame, posed in a rocking chair with one leg crossed perfectly over the other, his leather shoes gleaming. They must have dragged the chair out onto the lawn so there would be enough light. Bits and pieces of the house are in the background. And I also noticed, to tell the truth, that the old lady cheated even though we were only playing for a cent a point.

Everyone was glad to see John MacRae when he arrived at the church. Afterwards him and his suitcase got driven over to his sister's farm. Maybe they even took the picture that day. In the picture he is trying to look like a country squire on a mission of mercy.

At first things went pretty well. He and Tom Gorman never got to be friends but John MacRae was healthy enough to work and though he didn't do much he came in handy. He was still young, only thirty-two, and he let it be known that he had a little money in the bank and was just waiting around deciding where to buy.

John MacRae was what you could call a slow man. He had waited ten years to come back to the farm and after a while it looked like he might wait another ten before he got married and bought a place of his own. In the meantime he enjoyed himself. He did a few chores and he ate his sister's cooking. He constructed a huge sugar house to replace the old one that Tom Gorman and Billy Clenning's father had been using. Maple sugar, he said, was like money in the bank. There was nothing you could sell like maple sugar.

Down the road lived the widow Frank. She was just a bit older than John MacRae and it was thought that eventually he and she would see what was necessary and get together. The only person standing in the way was the young daughter of the widow Frank. About seventeen years old and pretty, she started to come visiting the Gorman farm. Not exactly officially but you could tell it was John MacRae she was after. He wasn't too old for her: he had city clothes and he had seen the world. Maybe she thought he would elope with her. Two years passed. John MacRae put on some weight and lost some teeth. His city clothes wore out and he didn't change his overalls from one week to the next. The pretty young Frank girl from down the road visited less often. She got married and moved away. He visited her mother, the widow Frank, a couple of times but his heart wasn't in it.

To console himself he ate. With everything he ate he had maple syrup or maple sugar. Pretty soon he was all stomach and hardly any teeth at all. His moustache grew wild and caught in his mouth when he was chewing. He spent so long over dinner that he hardly had time for an afternoon nap. The widow Frank told one of her neighbours that he was getting disgusting before his time, and that, as far as she was concerned, she didn't care if she never saw him again.

When the widow Frank announced that she was through with John MacRae she destroyed Tom Gorman's last hope for peace in his own house. He was so mad that if he hadn't been lame he would have kicked John MacRae from the house to the road. Not only was John MacRae eating twice as much as any normal man but he was teaching the children bad habits and driving his wife crazy.

This and more Billy Clenning told me as we moved on to the second bottle of the historic recipe. Of course people around here are terrible liars, the woman said. They've lied so much they've forgotten the truth. One time Pat Frank was at a wedding eating everything in sight. Someone asked him to play the fiddle. Well, he'd forgotten it. It's invisible, he said. Then for the rest of the day he walked around making noises like a bullfrog and trying to sing through his nose. Even to this day he won't admit he forgot it.

And that time she was telling me the truth because I asked Pat Frank about it, one day after he came home from the hospital. Oh no, he said, I didn't forget it. It had shrunk up and I had it in my pocket. He coughed. He was so thin, his cheeks had collapsed completely. He wasn't the same man at all, Mark said. No point trying to stop him drinking now.

Winters are always long in the country but John MacRae's last winter there was long indeed. When the weather's bad you are cooped up in the house and when it's good there's so much to do you can hardly enjoy it. In the morning, again at noon, then from dark until bed-time the family was in the kitchen. Probably John MacRae's picture was up on the wall even then. What must he have thought, looking at it? Perhaps he never bothered.

If the snow hadn't melted early they might not have been able to get into the bush to make syrup. But by March it was almost gone. Early that month John MacRae, glad to be out of the house and away from Tom Gorman, went out and tapped the trees: bored the holes in the bark and set in the narrow metal spiles. The weather stayed good and Tom Gorman and Billy Clenning's father went and got everything ready for boiling down the sap. The very most important step was to bring enough home-made wine to last the two men at least three weeks. During their annual drunk they cemented their friendship, prepared for the long summer ahead, and fed the fire inside the huge arch John MacRae had bought for the sugar house.

In those five unwanted years John MacRae had learned at least one thing. He had learned to stay out of the way when the serious drinking began. His job was to organize the kids, Billy Clenning included, into carrying the sap to the storage tank and splitting the wood. And while John MacRae stayed out of sight the two men, after spending a couple of days plotting to throw him out in the spring, forgot him and passed on to more pleasant topics. They even, and Billy Clenning heard them, said they might let him hang around another summer if he could be got to do a little work. After all he had built the big new sugar house and even if he was lying about the nest egg they were doing okay selling maple syrup every season. In fact, they admitted, they made more than twice as much as they ever had before the new house was built. And so it went. The women did what they had to and let the men be and the kids snuck in whenever they could to watch their fathers drink and swear.

One day, near the end, when the men had run out of wine and were roaming about, the old lady and John MacRae were in the sugar house alone. They were finishing off a batch of syrup and the sap was boiling away thick and hot. Suddenly there was the loudest scream you ever heard and the old lady, young then and John MacRae's sister, came running out of the shack shouting that Uncle John had fallen into the evaporator pan.

Well, Billy says, by the time he got there Uncle John was rolling around in the snow trying to get cooled off. When he stood up all the syrup had turned to taffy and Billy says he was the most amazing thing he ever saw. A big fat man standing up with a thousand strands of taffy coming out of everywhere and stretching, like a huge tent, right to the ground.

As it turned out, he survived. Tom Gorman and Billy Clenning's father cut the taffy off him with their pocket-knives and what the kids and dogs couldn't eat they broke into small peices and sold that summer at the church bazaar. He couldn't walk, they had to hitch up the horses and drag him home. Though he was badly burned he only complained once: that was when they cut off his moustache. A few weeks later he was better and except that he had turned a bit crazy, you wouldn't have known that it had taken two strong men four hours to cut him loose from his cocoon. But the experience had unstrung him. Fat and ugly as he was, he walked down the road one April day and proposed to the widow Frank right on her front steps. She invited him in, one thing led to another, and when he came out they were married by God and engaged by intent. But, like I said, John MacRae had turned a bit crazy. After a couple of days of being engaged he must have forgotten it had happened because the last anyone saw of him he was heading down the road at six o'clock in the morning, carrying his old suitcase and wearing his city suit. Whatever he'd come for he'd got.

In due course the twins were born. The widow Frank gave them her first husband's name and admitted that she was just as glad John MacRae had disappeared and, as far as she was concerned, she didn't care if she ever saw him again.

People round here are awful liars, the woman said. Now someone sooner or later is going to tell you that when John MacRae came out of the sugar house he said his own sister had pushed him in. He probably fell in drunk. Still, she said wistfully, you should have seen him when he came out. Just a big mountain of taffy, I guess he looked good enough to eat.

How do you know?

I was there, she said. I used to sneak around after Billy

Clenning.

In the fall Pat Frank died. After the funeral Mark Frank and I sat down in he cemetery to do whatever you do after a funeral. I wonder if you see anything when you're dead, he said.

I don't know. Right now I can hardly see a thing.

All you city people are the same.

Your nose is too long.

It is?

It's too long for the rest of your face. If it was a little longer it would be noble; if it was a little shorter it would fit in with the rest. But as it is, it's hopeless.

I never noticed it.

That's because you're crosseyed.

You know what? he said. You're right. I'm crosseyed from looking at my nose that's too long. I never knew it. How long do you think this has been going on?

It was the first thing I noticed.

And you never said anything?

No.

Soon we'll all be dead.

Soon enough.

Me, the old lady and Pat. There won't be anybody left at all.

No.

If old MacRae hadn't of been so crazy we'd have been dead long ago.

You wouldn't have been born.

He arced the bottle into the gravestone that had been waiting for that very moment, waiting for almost a century. It had been waiting so long it was half-toppled over and eaten away by doubt. The bottle crumpled against it and made a neat pile of glass. You know the old lady? he said. If I wasn't so dumb I would have killed her years ago.

JANICE

Assurance will be the means. I will walk into the room calmly, my weight well back and settled into myself. I will not notice her; she will not notice me. For a while, mutually oblivious, we will entertain ourselves with others. And then, at the exact accidental moment, we will come together, the three of us, and stand in a small triangle in the centre of the room.

"How are you, Robert?" she will say. She will speak to me as if I were a friend and put her hand on my arm. Not because she wants to tell me something but because she wants him to know that she can do that, put her hand on my arm confidently, meaninglessly. "How are you, Robert?" she will say, and then she will introduce me to him: "Robert, I would like you to meet Nicholas. We are going to be married in the fall." I will nod politely and express my congratulations. Perhaps she will, to settle everything, lean forward and kiss me lightly. Not because she wants to kiss me but because she wants to kiss me in public, show affection, be meaningless and confident with an old friend who has passed out of her life.

So that is how it will be. Brief, punctuated, and stylized. Nicholas will be reassured. He will make his small talk, offer me a cigarette, and then excuse himself to get us some drinks. We will be left standing there, in the middle of the room, wearing all of our clothes. Nicholas, because he does not yet know Janice, will not hurry himself. He will stand at the bar complacently, searching out the right brand of scotch and making sure that the ice cubes are the right size for the glass. It would never occur to him that the two people standing casually in the middle of the room, wearing all of their clothes, have never before spent an entire evening doing that, wearing all of their clothes.

"How are you, Robert?" she will say.

"Fine," I will reply. I'll look down at my feet, at her feet. Her feet will look peculiar to me wrapped in their shoes and stockings. I will remember her toes sticking out from under the flowered sheets of her bed, or, even more clearly, I will remember them tanned and drying in the sun, with little specks of sand on the insteps. Perhaps I will have a cigarette. The fact that I light the cigarette with the lighter I gave her, and she returned, will seem slightly melodramatic to her. It will make her feel contemptuous of my weakness, of my need to underline the situation.

* * *

Touch football became popular so Nicholas played water polo. He moved through the water with surprising grace. Smooth and hairless. One couldn't help thinking that he might have been injected with silicone. "Isn't he good," Janice said. She had moved close to me so that our thighs ran side by side.

"Oh yes," I agreed. "Excellent. It would be a pity to marry a man who couldn't swim." Nicholas stood at the edge of the pool, a towel draped around his shoulders. He was a beer advertisement who resembled a large Adonis. He was looking up at us, his face open and wet.

"They've decided it's half-time," Janice said. "Come down with me and talk to him." She stood up. My pants were glued to my leg by a thin line of sweat. She walked away from the bench where we had been sitting, walked over to Nicholas. Later, in the boathouse, she stripped off her jersey as if it were the most natural thing in the world, as if there were a social convention prohibiting jerseys in the boathouse. "Wait a minute," she said. She reached into her bag and pulled out a bikini top. "Well," she said when we were seated in the boat, "we can't just sit here."

"It's so hot in the sun," I said. "It would be so much cooler to stay here. We could take off all our clothes and make love in the rowboat."

She tried to smile at me but the smile slid down into her chin. She pushed the dock gently so that the boat was set in motion, gliding out of the shadows into the lake.

"Why did you come?"

"Why did you ask me?"

"It was Nicholas's idea. He said you looked so depressed at the party. He thought, you know, it might take you a while to get used to things."

I rowed out into the lake and across to a place where there were no cottages. There was a path leading up from the water to a little plateau. Lying on our stomachs we could barely see the heads bobbing up and down in the pool that had been built a few yards away from the lake. "It's just the same," she said.

"It always is."

"Why did you come?"

"I wanted to."

She giggled. "What would Nicholas think?"

"Nicholas has drowned. Didn't anyone tell you?"

* * *

"Nicholas is very clever with his hands," Janice said. Nicholas was standing in the middle of the room, a glass in each hand, juggling ice cubes.

"Perhaps he ran away with a circus."

"You should be grateful. Not everyone would be as understanding as Nicholas." She slipped her hand into my arm and extracted a ligament. "Look," she said, "now you've spilled your drink. I'll have to get you another one."

Nicholas had worked his way from two to three to four ice cubes. People were standing in a circle around him, clapping in time to the clicking of the ice against the glass. When he had all four ice cubes going well Nicholas sent the glasses into the air after them so that the room was filled with his act. Then he caught the glasses again and all the ice cubes clattered home, still cold and intact. I was disappointed. I had wondered if he could juggle water.

He went over and joined Janice at the bar. He put his hand on her shoulder and gave her a kiss. Later he will think how lucky he is that he has found someone like Janice, someone with intelligence and beauty bound together by an inner grace. He will ask himself again why she was attracted particularly to him and then will remember, anticipate, her passion with him, her praise of his strength. He will think that it is not only his special virtue that has brought them together but that there is something else – a fatedness, a chemistry, a unique bond that exists between them on some level more profound than words. Complacently, gratefully, he will turn out the lights and slide into bed with her. Now he was only talking to her. She nodded in agreement and came back to where she had left me. "It's time to go," she said. "Nicholas will wait for us in the car."

"Nicholas is very understanding."

She moved her hand over my face as if she thought that I had turned into a panda bear with a wet nose. "Come on," she said, "we haven't got all night."

* * *

"Don't worry," he said. "I won't hurt you." He moved around the ring easily, flicking his hand out occasionally, not making contact but pointing to the places where I had left myself open. He had insisted that I learn to box. It would improve my confidence. He assured me that athletics had made him over completely. "I used to be like you," he said. I was going for his nose and teeth. I would feint a punch to the body and then hit him in the face as hard as I could. Nicholas would move his arm lightly and brush away the punches. "You're trying too hard," he said. "Relax." I leaned against the ropes, wondering if I would bring up. Then we started again. I used the same strategy, feinting towards the stomach and then going for the face. His ribs were so well covered with flesh and muscle it was hard to know exactly where his diaphragm was. There is a place that is unprotected. When the pattern was nicely established, the feint and the punch, I estimated where it was and accomplished my revenge. "That's better," he said. "You're getting better all the time."

Standing in the shower I could feel the blisters on my feet raw against the tile. Nicholas, all friendliness, slapped me on the shoulder. "How about a swim?" he said. "The pool is very clean."

* * *

My shoulder was so sore I could hardly raise my arm. Janice knelt over me, tenderly licking it. "You see," she said, "when you're angry the only person you hurt is yourself."

"You're getting as bad as Nicholas."

"Nicholas thinks you don't like him."

"Nicholas is getting nervous."

"Nicholas is perfectly relaxed about everything."

"That's good. I think I'm getting an ulcer."

"Poor baby," she said. "Let momma kiss your tummy."

"Why don't you marry me?"

"I'm marrying Nicholas."

"What for?"

"If we were married would you let me see Nicholas?"

"No."

"What would you do if I saw him anyway?"

"I don't know," I said. "I guess I'd leave you."

"How touching."

* * *

We spent one summer in a cabin near a lake. There was no electricity so we went to bed early every night, sleeping on a porch that faced the sunrise. In the morning I would wake up to see the light lying flat and pink across our bodies. When I turned to her she was always awake. Not just waiting but lying there awake, as if she had no need of sleep or as if she had made the transition from night to day as easily and gradually as a cat. We would walk down to the lake in that early morning light, the grass still bright green with dew. And after we swam she would lie on the beach soaking up the sun, her body so still that when she got up the imprint was perfectly defined.

One night when I couldn't sleep, I woke her up and asked her to marry me. I don't know why I asked her, perhaps it was because everything between us had been flawless.

Perhaps it was because I was curious. She didn't answer me. She got out of bed and went outside. I sat up, lit a cigarette, and imagined being married to her. I will remember her as a series of images: her hair brushing against my shoulder, her eyes opening to me as I drink to her marriage, her tanned wet summer thighs. If we had lived together we would have had a room with a skylight. Our days and nights would have passed almost unnoticed. Our bodies would have stretched beyond our skins and ended in some galaxy that we never knew. If we had lived together we would have thought ourselves gods. It was at least possible.

"Robert," she said. "Do you still want to marry me?"

"No."

There was half a moon. Enough for us to see each other sitting in the grass watching the stars. She turned her head towards me and opened her eyes wide so I could look into them. I saw nothing. She might have been a witch. She might have been an ordinary woman sitting naked and beautiful under the late night summer sky.

* * *

Nicholas stood beside me on the balcony of his apartment. He smelled faintly of expensive cologne and toothpaste. "Robert," he said. He shifted his weight from one foot to the other, waiting for the opening. "Janice wanted me to ask you something . . . a favour. It isn't necessary, you understand . . . but I would like it too. . . It would be a kind of gesture. . . " He put his hand on my shoulder and looked at me directly, man to man. "We would like you to be the best man at our wedding."

"I would be delighted."

"Good," Nicholas said. "We hoped you would." He took his hand away and we turned again to face the city. He looked happy. It was the first time I had ever seen him look happy. "You know, Robert, when I look out at the city sometimes I wonder if everything is as it seems."

"Yes. There is always that question."

"No," he said, "I don't think you could know what I mean. You're too caught up in your own . . ." he wanted the exact word, the knockout punch, "unreality."

"I should have been a poet."

"No. You should have been a lawyer." He tugged his forelock. "Of course no one is perfect." Janice came out and joined us. "He's agreed," Nicholas said. "Isn't that wonderful?"

* * *

"How are you, Robert?" she will say. She will speak to me as if I were a friend and she will put her hand on my arm. It will be after the ceremony, we will be standing outside the church waiting for the cars to come and take us to the reception. "Did you notice the way the priest looked at us? He must have known everything." She will laugh.

"When are you leaving?"

"Not until tomorrow. We will want to wait a day, spend the first night here. I'm sure Nicholas will get drunk." Then she will squeeze my arm, turn to me, and kiss me lightly. Not because she wants to kiss me but because she wants to kiss me in public on the day of her wedding, show affection, be meaningless and confident with an old friend who has passed out of her life. "You will be here when we get back."

"Yes." All I will have to remember is to say yes to everything she asks, as if anything else were out of the question, as if it were bad manners to wear a jersey in a boathouse. Eventually they will find me but by then time will have intervened, turned us into old friends who were once intimate.

For the last time, on their wedding night, Nicholas will ask Janice about me. She will be standing in the kitchen of their apartment, naked, making orange juice for the morning. "Robert? I never could have married someone like Robert." She will take a long-stemmed rose and put it in the empty champagne bottle, in the centre of the kitchen table. Then she will walk into the bedroom and lie down on the bed. He will hear what she has said but he will not really hear it. The note of dismissal and finality in her voice will close the subject for him. He will think it is not only his special virtue that has brought them together but that there is something else – a fatedness, a chemistry, a unique bond that exists between them on some level more profound than words. Complacently, gratefully, he will turn out the lights and slide into bed with her.

* * *

When I woke up, the first thing I did was to look at the alarm. Ten o'clock. I got up and went straight for a cigarette. The place looked terrible. There was an ashtray dumped upside down in the bedroom. In the living room everything was as it had been left when the last person went home. There were glasses all over the place, ashes, butts and stains on the carpet. I went into the kitchen. Janice was sitting drinking coffee and staring out the window down at the parking lot.

"You look awful," she said.

"I feel it." I went and poured myself a glass of orange juice. "Who was that idiot juggling ice cubes in the living room?"

"Nicholas someone."

I finished the orange juice and started on the coffee. "Where did he come from?"

"He's staying with the people down the hall." She laughed. "I've forgotten their names too." She stood up and came over to me. "You *do* look awful." She kissed me lightly on the lips. She slid her hand into my arm and extracted a ligament. "Look," she said, "you've spilled half your coffee. I'll get you another cup, no, you get it, I think there's someone at the door."

* * *

They were playing water polo. Nicholas moved through the water determined but graceful. "Isn't he good," Janice said. She had moved close to me so that our thighs ran side by side.

"Oh yes," I agreed. "Excellent." Nicholas was resting at the edge of the pool. He was looking at us, his face open and wet.

"Let's go upstairs," Janice said.

"Here?"

"Why not? No one will mind."

Later, lying on the bed, we could hear the shouts and splashing from the pool. "You know," Janice said, "I like making love this way, unexpectedly."

"I saw you sneaking off with Nicholas."

"Don't be silly," she said. "I only do that with strangers."

THE TOY PILGRIM

THE TOY PILGRIM

Elmer was an unattractive child but he had a way with words. Outside of a few squeaks and burbles he said nothing at all until the age of two. Then he began to speak in perfect sentences and paragraphs. No-one was sure if Elmer's course of development was a sign of exceptional genius or of stupidity. With Elmer, despite his many accomplishments, such questions always remained valid.

Elmer was the fifth of five children and he regarded the world around him with a beatific misanthropy. Mrs. Elmer sometimes thought that Elmer's dour countenance was a reflection of his innate dissatisfaction with his position but Mr. Elmer thought it was God marking him for having named a child after himself.

Mr. and Mrs. Elmer were religious people and went to church every Sunday without ever missing. They were kind, generous, charitable and humble. With what was left over they did their best to be loving, reverent, gracious and virtuous. To a large extent they succeeded, and, what is more, passed on their own remarkable qualities to their children. With the exception of Elmer. Although Elmer was never greedy, nasty or selfish it was easy to see that he would like to be. Only the simultaneous lack of example and imagination forestalled it.

Elmer's three brothers and one sister led exemplary lives. In public school they stood fourth in their class. In high school the girl stood tenth but the boys stood first. All the boys took law and became lawyers. One turned to stocks and bonds, a second became a professor, the third went on to politics. They prospered and participated in the order of things. The girl married a scientist and served him with unblemished perfection.

Elmer, however, was continually less than was expected of him. But there was one outstanding exception. Mr. and Mrs. Elmer were very religious people. On a Sunday morning Elmer, at the age of one and a half, was carried in his mother's arms to hear for the first time the soft harmonies of the organ. Suddenly, in the midst of one of the hymns, he let out a loud shriek and then opened his eyes and gave his mother a look of such powerful clarity that she fainted right away.

That night she and Mr. Elmer discussed the matter at great length. Was it, they wondered, a sign of God's grace or more likely just a well-deserved reprimand? They decided to hope it wouldn't happen again and forgot the matter.

But the minister didn't. The next day he came round to pay a visit and inspect the child. After all, he pointed out, one shouldn't fear the unusual. If it weren't for the unusual the routine would be unbroken. Elmer, he said, was an unusual child. The Elmers agreed. That was precisely what they didn't like about Elmer. They found him unusual but not in an interesting way. In fact they found him somewhat distasteful. Of course they had felt guilty about this. One isn't supposed to find one's own child distasteful. But there was something about Elmer, something uneasy which made it permissible to feel distaste. Recognizing this, they ceased to feel guilty and treated Elmer just like any other distasteful child.

When Elmer was four he asked to be taught to read. "No," his father said. "You're too young to read."

"I don't care," Elmer said. "I want to learn to read. Then I can amuse myself and not bother you all the time."

"What's wrong with your Meccano set? Why don't you build a toy car or something?"

Elmer was disgusted. "The motor's broken and all the pieces are twisted. You didn't even buy me a new one. I don't like Meccano anyway. I want to read books."

"Alright," said his father. He went and got out the old Dick and Jane books and sat Elmer on his lap. He read through one slowly out loud, pointing to the words as he read.

When he was finished with the book Elmer climbed down off his lap. "Are all books like that?"

"Yes, more or less," Mr. Elmer said.

"Then I don't want to know how to read yet," said Elmer and he went off to try to build a toy car.

Being neither attractive, humorous or generous Elmer had a difficult time making friends and was relegated to the role of onlooker in neighbourhood play. Fortunately he was lumpy and forbidding and thus escaped being made a scapegoat. His parents were acutely grateful that Elmer was spared, a fortuitous event at best, they felt, and showed their gratitude by giving birthday parties for all the neighbourhood children. At these parties Elmer was silent and morose. It always seemed to be everyone else's birthday whereas his own came but once a year.

Elmer entered public school. The family relaxed. Although Mrs. Elmer had wanted to love him and sometimes felt real warmth towards him she found him a cold but demanding child and wondered why he had turned out that way.

In public school Elmer quickly learned how to read and was soon at the top of his class. Unlike his brothers Elmer was notably vain about being first and seemed to lack their sense of appropriate restraint. He had become a smug and complacent six year old. A look of immense satisfaction lingered obscenely on his face. He also had the habit of always being the first to wave his hand in the air when a question was asked and the teacher quickly tired of the sight of his pudgy gesticulating fingers.

Elmer's academic prominence made him the avowed enemy of the other males in the class. Consequently Elmer had to make a rather hurried exit from school. After a couple of months of his mother asking him why he didn't stay at school longer and play with the other children, Elmer weighed the relative hostilities and formed his plan. After school one day he managed to get out ahead of the others and hide behind a tree in the schoolyard. As usual his tormentors came outside and grouped in preparation for the daily sport of chasing Elmer home. When all their backs were turned Elmer emerged from behind the tree, lowered his head, and charged.

Before they knew what was happening Elmer had

bowled two of them over and was starting his second charge. This time he aimed at the biggest one and was himself dragged down by his target. The two of them rolled about in the gravel for a while, trying to fight, and then got tired. Elmer drew a packet of gum out of his pocket and offered everyone a stick.

When Elmer got home from school that night it was dark. His elbows and knees were scraped and his shorts were ripped. Mr. Elmer quickly surmised that Elmer had atoned for some of his sins and although he reprimanded Elmer for being so unChristian as to fight he also made sure that Elmer got an extra piece of pie for dessert.

The next day in school Elmer gave the wrong answer to three questions in the morning and didn't even put up his hand in the afternoon. After school Elmer hung around with his new friends for a while and then went home to his mother. She gave him a peanut butter and jelly sandwich and patted his head twice.

Elmer liked going to church. His family all sat in a row and Elmer sat at the end of the row; he had an aisle seat. He especially liked the organ music and when the organ played Elmer would remember how, when he was very young, God had walked right inside him and become part of him. When he went to church there was always the memory of that experience and Elmer wanted it to happen again. He was pretty sure it never happened to anyone else because no one ever said anything about it. At times he wondered if it was an ordinary occurrence and was never mentioned because it was so ordinary.

What finally convinced him it was unusual was compulsory Bible reading in public school. Elmer deduced from the Gospels that Jesus was exceptional because he had God's grace. One day he tucked the Bible under his shirt and took it home to read. He stayed up late and read all four Gospels carefully. He couldn't escape the conclusion that he too was God's Son and that he had some special mission to perform. The thought bothered him. He didn't want to be crucified.

The Bible said that anyone who believed could go to heaven so why should he have to be crucified to go there?

Elmer knew that he was very special in God's eyes and that he had a very special life ahead of him. One day, he knew, God would come inside of him forever and when that happened he would be God. When he thought about it, it made sense. After all God must get tired so he probably went inside people every now and then and let them be God for a while. Elmer figured that there were probably quite a few people who had been God but only Jesus had gotten famous. That was because he had *said* he was God and for saying that he had also been crucified. There was an obvious lesson and Elmer resolved never to tell anyone his secret lest the same fate befall him.

Sometimes at night Elmer would lie on his back in bed with his eyes open waiting for God to come inside him. Sometimes it would start to happen but Elmer would get scared and He would go away. This didn't worry Elmer; he knew that when the time was ripe it would all come to pass. In the meantime he had only to keep it quiet and carry on living.

There was only one person who suspected Elmer and that was the minister. Although Mr. and Mrs. Elmer had entirely forgotten the uncomfortable incident, the minister remembered it very clearly and kept his eye on Elmer when he was in church. Often, during the sermon, Elmer could see that the minister was talking directly to him as if to test him. This made Elmer uneasy and he would squirm in his seat and cough. It was essential that the minister not discover his secret: he would tell everyone and then Elmer would get crucified.

After church the minister would look Elmer straight in the eye and say, "Elmer, how are you?"

"Fine," Elmer would say. He didn't want the minister to see that he knew he was being watched because that might give away the secret. Once, while Elmer was standing with his parents talking to the minister, Elmer was sure the minister was about to betray him. He gave Elmer a sly look and started to talk. Elmer kicked him in the shins and ran.

It worked; the minister didn't tell. Elmer was severely spanked and sent to bed without supper but he considered the punishment minor compared to what could have happened.

After that the minister respected the God-force in Elmer and didn't stare at him so much during sermons. Perhaps, Elmer thought, he realised that Elmer was not yet old enough to assume his eventual burdens. Or perhaps he even considered that the kick in the shins was sufficient proof that Elmer wasn't special after all.

That was fine with Elmer. He knew that he and God could bide their time together.

After the preliminary adjustments Elmer had to make in Grade One he had a reasonably happy existence until one night, at the age of eleven, while undressing, he noticed three darkish hairs growing near his penis. This occasioned a thorough inspection during which he found several suspicious looking hairs on his legs and a definitely black coarse hair in his right armpit. He went into the bathroom and looked at his sideburns. Yes, it was true, they were getting longer. Also the moustache that he had imagined for years was slowly becoming a reality.

Puberty meant trouble and Elmer knew it. He had read it in one of his mother's women's magazines. Not only had he read about it but he had seen his brothers and sisters pass into it and it had had, on each of them, a discernibly negative effect.

His sister, who had never liked him but who had at least left him alone, had become cross with him when her turn came and had started to criticize him for all sorts of faults, real and imaginary. She exuded mystery and importance and withdrew her affection from all her brothers.

To Elmer the explanation was simply a fall from Grace. As far as sexual data were concerned Elmer had taken the precaution of reading the relevant sections of the encyclopaedia and was, in his own estimation, fully informed as to the biological mechanics of the situation. He once remarked to his sister, who was scurrying to the bathroom with a kotex tucked under her blouse, that there was nothing unique about menstruation and that she ought to accept it as the course of Nature. His sister contented herself with slapping his face and locking the bathroom door.

But when confronted with the signs of his own hairy fallibility he felt a definite panic. Of course Elmer didn't want to remain eleven years old forever. He was most definitely looking forward to being bigger and even to leaving home. Nonetheless the thought of going through a gawky adolescence had so little appeal for him, especially since he'd witnessed his brothers making fools of themselves, that his faith in his own pact with God wavered. After all, it had been of the essence that God might enter him at any moment whatever. It was that certainty which had given meaning to his daily life. But how could God enter him, how could He want to, if he became asymmetrical and pimply, with hairs growing unevenly from his armpits?

* * *

During his first two years of university Elmer's parents paid his tuition but Elmer otherwise supported himself by working in the summer for one of his brothers and by waiting on tables and tutoring high school students in the winter. At the beginning of his third year, after his first night back waiting on tables, Elmer went home to think. He was living in the back room of the second floor of a rooming house.

The room had a bed, a desk and bookshelves above it, a dresser and an armchair. When he moved in Elmer had painted the walls of the room white and had bought pennants to hang on the walls. He was very proud of his room and hoped to take pictures of it before the year was out. The best feature of the room was the window looking onto the back yard. From the window he could see two big trees. He could also climb through the window onto a fire escape and thus make exits or entrances at any time of the day or night. Undetected. No one cared when he came or went but one never knew. Besides, Elmer was twenty years old and more than ready for nocturnal involvements with the fair sex.

Elmer sat down in his armchair and thought about waiting on tables and tutoring high school students. They were both occupations he disliked. It occurred to him that he ought to be able to use his ingenuity to avoid such labours. He could, of course, have borrowed money to go to university but that would only commit him to further penury after graduation. He also could have worked harder and tried to win big scholarships but since grade school Elmer's level of performance had dimmed to the point where he was lucky to be awarded enough money to buy his books.

He considered his position. Twenty years old. A third year student in English and Philosophy. He had no marketable talent whatever. He picked up a magazine and started flipping through it. He became absorbed in a short story about a young man who sold automobiles. Then it hit him. Of course. He should have done it years ago. First he would need a pen-name. Harold. Elmer had always wanted to be named Harold. Harold Noteworthy. Noseworthy. Groteworth. Noteworth. Harold Noteworth. He took a pen and pad and began to write.

> *The young woman raised her long curled lashes and centred her liquid eyes on the face of the handsome young man standing in front of her.*
>
> *"Oh," he said. "Hello. Haven't I met you somewhere before?"*
>
> *"You're awfully handsome," she said. "What's your name?"*
>
> *"Elmer," he replied, his sensuous lips framing the word.*

It was three in the morning before Elmer finished the first draft of his story. The next day he went out and bought a second-hand typewriter for twenty-five dollars. It took him three days to type out the story. He put it in a nice brown envelope and sent it off. Then he went to the bank and opened an account under the name of Harold Noteworth. Of course, there were problems. Suppose he won the Nobel Prize for literature. Would he reveal his true name or stand by his anonymity? It was a difficult question. He should have sent in the story under his own name. But if he had done that then he would have had to call the hero Harold. Elmer was a much more resonant name.

Having confirmed his decision, Elmer sat down to start writing his second story. He thought he could easily write a story a week. At a thousand dollars a story that would give him fifty thousand a year. Even with taxes he would be left with a fair sum. He decided to study the stock market as soon as he had some spare time.

> *The ocean pounded the ragged coastline. The wind howled. It was only twenty degrees above zero. All along the shore the people waited, lanterns in hand, to see if anyone would emerge. Finally, a cry was heard above the pounding of the surf.*
>
> *"There he is," Jack shouted. "There he is and he's got her too." The crowd heaved a collective sigh of relief and rushed out to help him in. Elmer struggled out of the water, cradling the pale Dorothea to his chest as if to protect her from the brutal wind. When they were finally out of the reach of the arms of the sea Elmer collapsed on the beach, exhausted by his prodigous feat. But before he passed out Dorothea managed to press her soft lips to his ear and whisper "Elmer, how can I ever thank you?"*
>
> *The End*

Elmer folded up his second story, placed it in a brown

envelope, and went outside to mail it. He was incredibly tired. He decided not to write any more until he had received results from the first two stories.

Two weeks later Elmer had his first rejection slip. It was a fine printing job on expensive bonded paper and Elmer tacked it up on the inside of his cupboard door. He went out and bought ten dollars worth of cheap magazines that carried fiction and read them over carefully, trying to determine what it was that characterised the short stories. His second rejection was a personal letter saying that if he could pare down his prose the editors would pay him seventy-five dollars for his story. Elmer dutifully revised his story and mailed it back. He also put three more into production.

By Christmas Elmer had six more stories out at magazines. He also had a cardboard box full of old pocket books and newspapers to which he would refer for plot ideas and stylistic inspiration. Harold Noteworth had hit the market. Elmer deferred contemplations about the Nobel Prize and concentrated instead on growing a moustache. To celebrate his good fortune he wrote his parents saying he couldn't go home for Christmas and bought a bottle of scotch to share with his friends. A certain young lady, a Carolyn, had recently been encouraging his advances and Elmer, although he had not told her anything about his enterprise, was sure his success had provided him with an enigmatic magnetism.

* * *

Elmer glided the metal nail file back and forth across his fingernails, barely carressing the adjacent skin. If anyone had walked in and asked him why he was filing his fingernails in this particularly narcissistic manner he would have disdained to reply and returned with total concentration to his task.

He sat in a dark brown rocking chair, rocking beside his light green radiator. On the top of the radiator were stacked three shelves of science fiction books, seven ashtrays, two empty packs of cigarettes, an alarm clock, a crumpled up piece of paper with the phone number of a girl he had met at a restaurant, and a leather button. The night before he had gone to see a movie but had thrown away the stub.

He lived in a square attic room with green walls and uncomfortable radiators. Being wholly unemployed and otherwise unoccupied he had the leisure and initiative to keep his nails in trim and clean them under the tips three times a day.

Elmer was not, however, an amorphous being, a member of anyone's imaginary mass, nor even an undifferentiated portion of the Godhead. No. Elmer had a higher ambition and purpose. Seated in his rocking chair, stroking himself mechanically, Elmer was a self-conscious one-man vanguard of destiny. Elmer, in fact and fancy, was a writer.

People seldom asked Elmer what it meant to be a writer. For one thing his appearance belied his intellect. Shaggy eyebrows, low-cut straight black hair, tubby: Elmer was far from prepossessing. Nonetheless he had, as he himself was open enough to recognise, a certain stability in figure and movement, a modest lack of grace that indicated the dignified understatement which was the clearest theme of his existence.

His face, neither rugged nor round, was shaped gently, its perfect smoothness spoiled only by a few patches of stubble. After filing each of his nails Elmer walked over to his bed and pulled an electric razor out from under his pillow. He plugged it into the socket and shaved. When he was finished he ran his fingers lightly over his cheeks and neck to make sure everything was as it should be. Satisfied with his shave, Elmer replaced his razor and sat down again in his rocking chair.

The raindrops slid down his window. Elmer pressed his nose against the glass and peered out at the people walking up and down the street. Criss-cross, their paths criss-crossed like chicken tracks, leaving no trace at all.

The sky was shiny grey and Elmer put on his sunglasses to protect his eyes from the rainbow. He looked at the house across the street. There was a window with a drawn curtain.

It had green, white and blue stripes. Behind the curtain Helga was lying on the bed fantasising about Elmer. She imagined him putting on his jacket and coming into her house. She wanted to hear his feet on the stairs. The thought of his bushy eyebrows was driving her insane. She wanted to go to the window and look out at Elmer. No. That would be too obvious. She relaxed and sent out mental pulses to him. The energy would arrest him in his tracks, paralyze him, drench his brain with images of desire.

Elmer took off his sunglasses; they were getting fogged. His heart beat faster. He was sure that Helga was sending signals to him from across the street. He could phone her. He thought of phoning her. He would dial her number and let it ring twice. Surely she would answer. If she didn't answer it would mean she knew it was him and he should come right over. He remembered he hadn't changed his socks for three days. How could he go to her with dirty socks? He pulled a cardboard box from under his bed and rifled through it. No socks. Hanging from a nail on the wall was a green cotton laundry bag. It had ELMER stitched in red letters across it. Inside Elmer's laundry bag were his socks. They were all dirty.

Helga lay on her bed. Her eyes were tightly shut and there were beads of sweat on her forehead. Elmer forgot about his socks and clambered down the stairs, out the door and across the street. His knees were weak with lust as he hurled himself up the stairs of Helga's house, through the front door and finally into her room. Mad with frenzy they consummated their two-ness.

Elmer and Helga got married. The sun was a yellow disc burning up the blue sky. It was June. Helga wore a white taffeta gown and silver pumps. Elmer wore a rented tuxedo and black patent leather wellington boots. They had cloth insets and little cloth loops at the back to help him pull them on.

Elmer's parents came to the wedding. Everyone was surprised to see his parents. Elmer wasn't the type of person to invite his parents anywhere, least of all to his wedding. They were very uncomfortable. Mr. Elmer and Mrs. Elmer pretended to be proud but really they were just embarrassed to be identified as the parents of someone like Elmer. They shuffled and sweated and smiled throughout. When it was over they went back to their motel and drank a bottle of rye. Then they made love for the first time in two months. Afterwards Elmer's father wiped his face with his shirtsleeve and remarked that weddings were a tonic.

Helga's parents came to the wedding too. They were blond and young-looking. They paid for the wedding and rented a pastor with a modest church and a short sermon. The pastor had lanky hair and a quiet way of intoning the verities. The friends were all pleased with the modest good taste and resolved to go to church again sometime. Privately Elmer thought that the whole thing was ridiculous but he knew that Helga would feel happier. Helga felt worse. Living in sin with Elmer was fine but she didn't think he was the type of man one would marry. Not that she had anything against Elmer but he offended her sense of propriety. Still, Elmer would gain a sense of psychological security that he had obviously missed at home and would, when the time came, be able to pay for the divorce. He might even be good for some alimony.

After the wedding Elmer and Helga sailed away in a wooden ship to Belgium where they set up a shop selling yard goods and had seven blond children. Subsequently Elmer left Helga and travelled through Europe telling everyone the sad tale of his life. Seated in a dark bar at midnight, he would inflict his story on any passing stranger. Soon he became known as a bore and no-one would hear him out even in a strange city. Thereafter he drank himself to sleep. When he woke up the minister was asking him if he would take Helga as his lawful wedded wife.

"Yes," he said. It was too late to say no. It was agreed then. They were married. Elmer was twenty-four years old. Helga was twenty-one. Her skin was white and clear and her breasts were round and firm. Beneath each breast was a fault line indicating its future course and there was a faint wisp of blond hair just below her belly. At night she slept soundly and when she woke in the mornings she smiled cheerfully. Her hands were nicely formed and her thighs were strong and warm. Elmer considered himself lucky to have gotten such a wife but wished she were a better cook.

He especially adored her mind. He considered it clear, pink and unbroken. In fact Helga's mind was filled with deep shadows and ruminations of which neither of them were aware. She was a latent psychopath and proved it by shoplifting a set of dishes every Thursday. As a result of one of these episodes she ended up seeing a psychiatrist. "You have penis envy," he told her. Then he gave her a big bright red pen and sent her home. Helga ceased her shoplifting but could often be observed chewing thoughtfully at the tip of her pen.

So be it. Elmer and Helga were married unbeknownst to each other on a bright June day. After their marriage they drove a rented car to Niagara Falls. They paid twenty-five cents and watched the water rushing mindlessly over the rocks into deep and resounding whirlpools. Illumined by floodlights, it presented them with an unparallelled vista of swirling energy and beauty. They copied it all down and took it back to the hotel where Elmer initiated his new bride into the Tantric rites which provide both birth control and ecstasy.

In the morning Helga noticed that Elmer had some black hairs on his back. Had she known he had black hairs on his back she never would have married him. She got a pair of tweezers and started to remove them. Her mother had told her, on the eve of her wedding, that marriages aren't made in heaven but have to be worked on. She had just cleared a small patch when Elmer woke up. Shutup Elmer, she said. I want to squeeze your blackheads.

Elmer cut off his soliloquy and held his breath for twenty-four hours.

* * *

In the mornings Elmer slept late. Off their bedroom was the study where he wrote his comic plays and the occasional detective novel. He liked to lie awake in bed in the morning and smoke cigarettes and remember his perfect writer's childhood. The incident in the church had stayed with him. Everything else was fluid. He might have been brought up by an old couple who found him in their garden. Sometimes he fancied himself a European emigre; English was his third language and his writing distinguished itself by appearing as if translated. Of course it had been a struggle to learn the language. He could remember distinctly the awkward moments in the subway station, the look of bewilderment on the faces of the young women he had courted. In all the versions of his life he had overcome initial handicaps to achieve his final status. Even in the athletic incarnation, the one in which he excelled at hockey, he had been forced to accept his physical mortality and strive for a more permanent art.

In his favourite story he had been slow in school. For years he had slipped from grade to grade, always at the bottom of his class. Finally a teacher, an old spinster woman who collected china teacups, had recognized him. She had brought him to her house from school twice a week and read him extracts from Proust and Dickens. At first it had been difficult. He had squirmed in his satin chair and stretched out the cookies desperately. But slowly the innate being in him had emerged to grasp what was being offered. After two or three months he started to ask to take books home. He would read them secretly in his windowless room by the light of a tallow candle. The later scholarships and success had gratified him but it was to that first teacher he credited everything. Before he became famous, while he was still writing short stories for women's magazines, he would go to visit her grave in the cemetery once a week. Perhaps he had even bought her a wreath with his first check. He resolved to dedicate his next novel to her. People would ask him what it meant but he would say nothing and keep her memory perfect and intact.

He lay in bed unresistant to the late morning light. Despite the money, the unlisted telephone number, the occasional recognition on the street, the two bright and well-behaved children, Elmer couldn't help but feel he had been betrayed. Surely God had not walked into him just in order to make him rich or famous. But the larger purpose was intangible to him. He liked to imagine that he would finally leave Helga and become a pilgrim. Walking down the street early one morning he would feel a curious sense of release. He would feel that his whole life was at once behind him and ahead of him. He would feel that day and night had come together in him. He would walk down the street and out of the city until he came to a place by the highway where he could sit. He would be picked up by a strangely beautiful girl in an ordinary car. She would take him somewhere, somewhere far away, where he would sit under a tree and meditate. He would grow gaunt. His eyes would burn. His spine would become a conduit of energy. He would experience unspeakable suffering and profound joy. The sun would explode in an infinity of golden drops and ten thousand buddhas would dance light and shadows across the windswept grass. He would pass from the world and re-enter the stream of the living. There would be no reprisals.

He lay in bed in the morning light. When he was young he had been a musician. He had heard the music of the spheres and had passed from childhood to adulthood as easily as a symphony. A violin concerto. An aria. It had all been so perfect for him, always. There had never been an awkward moment in the attic, a marriage to a woman who didn't exist for him, a career based on vanity and ambition. Right from the moment when he was one and a half years old, a babe in his mother's arms, the moment when God had entered him, He had never left him.

Elmer got out of bed and looked in the mirror. His full-fleshed face was beginning to sag. There were bags under his eyes and his thick black hair was dry and lifeless. He looked into his eyes and saw tiny red veins. There were lines on his forehead. When a man reaches forty he is responsible for his own face. He would soon be forty. Another few years. Already he was having his suits specially tailored. God was betraying him with time, betraying him again as He had originally betrayed him.

Elmer pulled on his pants and went into the bathroom to shave. His shoulders were sloped and rounded. He didn't like to look at them. Nor did he enjoy looking at Helga any longer. She had thickened, drooped and faded. Her blond hair was turning brown and she had the beginnings of a moustache. He remembered everything. He remembered that his sister had scurried from her bedroom to the bathroom with a Kotex tucked under her blouse. Soon Helga would be barren. He remembered that his brothers had all become successful before him. Occasionally there were family reunions: the Elmer clan gathered sleek and ageing in the parental home. Wine was drunk. There were no toasts.

He went into the kitchen and poured himself a glass of orange juice. The artist, having overcome childhood disasters and obstacles, finally fulfills his innate promise. But at the very moment of his greatest success, at the exact height of his fulfillment, it is soured by the taste of truth. He realizes that he has reached the top of the hill only to face the abyss on all sides. He drinks himself to death. Or he jumps in front of a car. Or he buys a railroad. Or he cultivates his irony and controls his breathing. Decades of emptiness stretch ahead. Even new triumphs will only prove that God has deserted him. Elmer plugged in the electric kettle and contemplated his boils.

He sat down at the kitchen table and looked out over the patio to his swimming pool. Helga had told him recently that he looked like a porpoise when he lay on the rubber raft in the swimming pool. Occasionally she still clung to him but she had ceased to moan.

> *There had been a curious incident. Elmer's parents, deeply religious people, had always taken their children to church. One Sunday morning, at the age of one and a half, Elmer was carried in his mother's arms to hear for the first time the soft harmonies of the organ. Throughout the service he dozed until suddenly, in the midst of one of the hymns, he let out a loud shriek and then opened his eyes and gave his mother a look of such clarity that she fainted right away. Though the rest of his life had faded the memory of that morning stayed with him. Elmer, seated beneath a tree in a windswept field, was finally able to draw a straight line between that fateful moment and the present. He lost himself in compassion and let his body dissolve into pure being. Elmer passed from the world.*
>
> *The End.*

Elmer got up from the table and paced back and forth in the kitchen. In his mind he had the plot for his next comic play. It would be about a man perpetually embarassed by himself. As for the novel, he would write it secretly and specify that it be published only after his death. It would be the only work to be published under his own name. He looked out the kitchen window. The abyss had disappeared and was replaced by a swimming pool. The sun exploded in an infinity of golden drops and ten thousand buddhas danced across the surface of the water. He closed his eyes and felt that God was within him.

Helga came into the kitchen. She was carrying a basket of pomegranates. "Elmer," she said. "I didn't know you were awake."

He turned to her in the noonday light. "Yes," he said. It was as if he was seeing her for the first time. Every detail was clear to him. He took one of the fruits and bit deeply into it. He chewed the red pulp slowly, savouring its slightly acid taste. He stored the seeds in a corner of his mouth and then spat them into an ashtray.

"Elmer," she said. "How many times do I have to tell you not to be such a pig."

UNCLE PHILBERT AND HIS BIG SURPRISE

Cast (in order of appearance):

Aunt Sally: A friendly and capable woman in her mid-thirties, with expressive voice and hands.

Mary: An outgoing, fun-loving girl. Eight years old. Very impulsive, she sometimes has to be restrained.

Jane: A quite withdrawn girl, a bit younger than Mary. She is socially mature for her age and is very creative.

Ronny: A typical ten year old boy, on the verge of puberty, who alternates between insecurity and confidence.

Uncle Philbert: A big brusque man in his early forties who brims with a zest for life and adventure. He has the energy and certainty that children love.

The opening scene takes place in Aunt Sally's living room. There are the usual props: a couch, a couple of armchairs, shelves with toys and materials on them, a tea pot.

AUNT SALLY:

Well children, I have a surprise for you today. Your Uncle Philbert is coming to visit.

MARY AND JANE
(together):

Oh boy, Uncle Philbert is coming. You told us about him and now he's coming. Do you think he'll bring us any presents?

AUNT SALLY:

Now girls.

JANE:

Yes Mary, we had better be good or we won't get our presents.

RONNY:

I hope he brings me something special.

AUNT SALLY
(smiling):
Really, you children act as if you never get anything. Don't you remember what you got for Christmas?

MARY:
I remember. It broke.

JANE:
And I remember who broke it.

RONNY:
I did not. It fell apart. It was only a doll anyway.

AUNT SALLY:
And do you remember that we made Mary a new doll out of paper maché? It was all decorated with stars and stripes and it had a nice little dress.

JANE:
I made the dress.

RONNY:
Look. Look out the window. Look at Uncle Philbert. He's got a great big shiny car and he's coming up the sidewalk. And his arms are full of parcels. Oh boy.

AUNT SALLY:
Now children, be calm. Sit down on the sofa with your hands folded and I'll go to the door and greet your Uncle Philbert.

JANE:
Yes, let's sit quietly.

MARY:
Yes, sit down Ronny.

RONNY:
I wanna go out and see his car.

AUNT SALLY
(smiling):
You can see the car later, dear. Maybe if you are very good your Uncle Philbert will take you out for a ride.

The doorbell rings. Aunt Sally smiles one last time at the children and goes to open the door. Enter Uncle Philbert.

UNCLE PHILBERT
(expansively):
Hi kids. It's great to see you. I'm your Uncle Philbert.

MARY, JANE, and RONNY:
Hi, Uncle Philbert.

AUNT SALLY:
Hello Uncle Philbert.

They shake hands.

UNCLE PHILBERT
coming up to the sofa, parcels still in his arms:
Well, what a surprise this is. It just happens that I have three big presents here. Now. Which one of you is Mary?

MARY:
I am.

UNCLE PHILBERT:
Pleased to know you, Mary. I haven't seen you since you were a little baby. Here's something I brought you from my visits to Wild Africa.

MARY:

Oh boy.

She tears at the tissue paper.

AUNT SALLY:

Say thank you, Mary.

MARY:

Thank you.

UNCLE PHILBERT:

And you must be Jane.

Jane:

Yes Uncle Philbert.

UNCLE PHILBERT:

Here you are Jane. I hope you enjoy this.

Meanwhile Mary has gotten her parcel unwrapped. The present is a long recorder-like instrument.

MARY:

What's this?

UNCLE PHILBERT:

Just a moment, Mary. First I have to give Ronny his present. Now, Ronny, this is for you.

RONNY:

Thank you, Uncle Philbert.

Mary has put the recorder to her mouth and is starting to make noises on it. Jane unwraps her present and discovers that it is a washboard. Ronny's present is a bow with rubber-tipped arrows. The two girls experiment with their new toys while Ronny fidgets with his bow and arrow.

AUNT SALLY:
Well, what nice presents Uncle Philbert has brought you. Why don't you play a little song?

Mary starts playing "Three Blind Mice" on her recorder while Jane bangs her washboard. They are just finishing the first verse when Ronny shoots Mary with a rubber tipped arrow.

MARY:
Ow!

She jumps on Ronny and starts pounding him with her fists.

AUNT SALLY:
Ha Ha. What fun presents you brought, Uncle Philbert. Why don't you take Ronny outside with the bow and arrow while I teach the girls how to play the national anthem?

UNCLE PHILBERT:
Yes, Aunt Sally. What a good idea. Come with me, Ronny, and I'll teach you how to hunt wild rhinoceroses.

RONNY:
Oh boy!

Uncle Philbert and Ronny exit and re-emerge at the edge of a jungle clearing in deepest Africa. In the clearing are a variety of exotic wild animals, grazing, drinking at a spring, romping about aimlessly. Ronny has with him his bow with rubber-tipped arrows. Uncle Philbert carries no weapons save a movie camera and a boy-scout hunting knife. They are crouched behind a fallen banana tree.

Ronny is visibly nervous and Uncle Philbert is trying to reassure him.

UNCLE PHILBERT

Drawing his knife from his sheath and running his thumb along the blade:

Don't worry 'bout that, boy. I can take care of us.

RONNY:

It sure is nice here.

UNCLE PHILBERT

In the jungle he is more masculine, more self-assertive than he was at Aunt Sally's:

Yup. A man's a man here. Now you listen to me, boy. See that thingamabob over there skulking around them ferns? Now when it comes close to us you let him have it. Right between the eyes.

RONNY

scared:

Okay. B-but how do I know when to shoot?

UNCLE PHILBERT:

When you see the whites of his eyes. Now get your arrow ready and don't ask any more fool questions.

While they wait, Uncle Philbert pares his nails with his hunting knife. Periodically he emits a low moaning whistle, obviously designed to attract their prey. The animal they are stalking is a large but graceful stuffed donkey covered with purple velvet. It has button eyes, large floppy ears, and a tail with a luxurious tassle at the end. As it moves around, grazing and nuzzling the grass, its ears wave in the breeze.

RONNY:
I like him.

UNCLE PHILBERT:
Hm.

RONNY:
Why do I have to shoot him?

UNCLE PHILBERT:
Well boy, that's a good question. Why do you have to shoot him? Yup. Well. You know Ronny, when I was about your age, maybe a little younger, my uncle took me on my first safari. Told me I wouldn't be a man if I couldn't kill. Yup. He was a tough old bugger, he was. Skin like sandpaper and hair growing out of his nose. Yup. He said you gotta kill to be a man. Well I didn't think that was right, I said you don't have to kill to be a man. You just have to be honest, forthright and clean and have a good sense of humour and work hard. Well boy, he looked at me and roared. Bullswog, he shouted. *BULLSWOG*. Well he shouted so loud that the herd of elephants we was stalking came running full tilt right at us. I hid behind a tree and my uncle stepped out, all he had was an old Lee Enfield, and let them have it. Yup. He just fired right at them. Well, you should have seen them. They turned right around and ran off just as fast as they could go. But he'd got one. Yup. Great big hairy elephant with tusks ten yards long lay dead in the middle of the clearing. And you know what my uncle did then? He walks right up to it, squatts down, tears it apart and eats it with his bare hands! Yup. Ate the whole thing. Even ate the bones. Never seen a man eat so much before or since. Yup. Now let me tell you something boy. Compared to when I was a kid this is just a runthrough. Chickenshit. By the time I was your age I had massacred whole zoos of animals. And I ain't half the man my uncle was. And he weren't even a quarter the man *his* uncle was. You know who that was, boy? *Buffalo*

Bill. Single-handed he wiped out every buffalo on the western plains. Killed them all til it was clean as a whistle, the old Indian. Yup. Ain't no hundred men today could stand up to a man like that. Nope. Somebody goes hunting now they want to take a goddamn atomic arsenal with them. Cannons, hand grenades, land mines. You know what that is? That's *chickenshit.* Yup. A real man would chew something to death if he had to.

RONNY:

Wow!

UNCLE PHILBERT:

Now it's coming close boy. Get yourself ready to let him have it.

Ronny stares at the donkey as it grazes closer and closer. When it is only a few feet away it lifts its head and stares straight into Ronny's eyes. He looks at the eyes; they are hazel green and translucent like the eyes of a cat. But around the green pupils is a thin white rim. He releases the arrow. The suction cap catches the donkey right on the forehead and throws it into the air. It falls on its side on the ground with a loud thud. The arrow is still quivering as Ronny and Uncle Philbert come out from behind their log to inspect their prize. When they are close to the donkey it rolls over on its back, its legs sticking up into the air, and begins to bellow. The other animals, hearing the death agonies of the donkey, move away slowly, leaving Uncle Philbert, Ronny and the dying donkey in the centre of the clearing. The donkey's cries grow louder and louder. Ronny puts his hands over his ears but can't help watching. The donkey begins to bleed; a great geyser of blood comes up from it, drenching Uncle Philbert and Ronny. At first

Ronny is too astonished to react. Then he breaks down, rolling on the ground screaming and crying. Uncle Philbert, meanwhile, stands happily in the midst of things. He is smiling ecstatically. One might think that he had just discovered oil. The force of the bleeding gradually increases. The sound of the blood spattering on the ground begins to drown out Ronny's crying. Finally the donkey explodes.

UNCLE PHILBERT

shouting above the noise:

Come on Ronny, now's the best part.

He grabs Ronny by the hand and drags him towards the donkey.

Just dive right in boy, dive right in.

Ronny and Uncle Philbert are shown in a campfire scene. It is later the same day. They are both still spattered in blood and are wearing various bandages, slings, etc. Ronny has a blood-stained bandage wrapped around his head but looks peaceful and contented.

RONNY:

Boy, Uncle Philbert, that was really fun today. Thank you for taking me hunting and making me a man. Boy, am I ever full.

Ronny wipes his mouth and burps.

UNCLE PHILBERT:

That's alright boy. Next week I'll show you some real action. And *don't pick your nose.*

STRAIGHT POKER

It would be foolish to ignore everything that is known in favour of speculation. I can tell you her eyes are brown. Sometimes they change colour but still, they are brown. That is one thing that is known.

But the first thing I wanted to know was whether we would touch. How would it be? I am a practical man. She doesn't care. She knows that everything is literal. She has perfect breasts. I have flat feet. She is graceful and walks through our rooms like a cloud. A stream down a mountain. Any one of those things. I am charming every second Wednesday. I tell lies. I stay up late at night and write letters to non-existent friends.

Life is like climbing a mountain blindfolded, I said. We sat on the floor and drank tea. I come to her at different hours of the day and night seeking myself. I am a practical man. On that subject she is neutral but compassionate. The contracts are torn up as quickly as they are renewed.

Life is like climbing a mountain blindfolded, I said. She looked at me as though I was out of my mind. We were sitting on the floor drinking tea. The afternoon sun came in the window. I take sugar in my tea and smoke tobacco. She is tolerant. The first time we touched it was almost an accident. Our hands brushed as we were crossing a street. Now we are covered with bits of each other's flesh.

We have lived in many places. Each place is different. They share many things but they are different. All the physical details must be incorporated. For example: there was one place with green paint peeling from the kitchen cupboards. Another example: we lived in a cottage with a full basement. The man who owned the cottage came and trimmed the cedar hedge every Sunday. It was not a good relationship and ended with us circling in the yard, each trying to keep the sun at his back. But that summer the lake was clear and cold and so calm at evening that we often canoed into the sunset.

I used to ask her to tell me she loved me. I love you, she would say. You're just saying that, I would say. What do you expect? I don't know what I expected. I must have been hoping for something. At least that's what I thought.

Some sentiments come easily. Like filling small buckets of sand on the beach and carrying them about. Like a stream flowing down a mountain.

* * *

Some things are known. That much is certain. I have never met you yet we are well acquainted. But not old friends. We are not meant to be old friends with each other. At times it seems impossible that we will ever be truly intimate. There is so much that meets on the surface that I wonder how we will ever get past it. It is easy to see that you think you already know me. You send me messages of condolence and telegraph flowers. What do you hope I will do with a dozen daisies in February? It is leap year but I will refuse to marry you.

She hasn't seen you yet but I know you are there, looking in the windows and taking my measure. It doesn't matter. I look in your windows too. We look in each other's windows: FIRE SALE the signs say but we both know better. Despite everything it could still happen.

It irritates you when I enumerate the possibilities. You want to be open. You want to let things happen as they may. Yet you have already calculated everything. Does it surprise you when I say that? I see that it doesn't. I can't imagine your body at all.

I know you will not forgive me if I see you as an iron mother. And so I tell you there will be nothing to be forgiven. I will imagine your body after all, slender and white moving across hotel beds with perfect grace. It is too soon for betrayal.

We have a mutual friend. Every morning she wakes up and creates the universe. We are not within her power yet we fear her. It is irrational and we will soon forget it. We will forget it in a bedroom compartment of a train travelling at seventy miles an hour across the prairies. All the other evidence is immaterial.

It is necessary to be realistic. Our bodies are poised between youth and middle age. There are scars, knots of muscle. There are soft spots that have come and gone. There are details that were appropriated by others intent on their own purposes. There is much to be overcome, Many former ecstasies to be gathered in by our tentative passion. We may never meet.

* * *

We come to each other at different times of the day and night. At dawn I felt her curled around me, her hand tracing patterns on my chest and stomach. Last week, when I was asleep, she drew a flower on my knee. When I woke up she was gone. I could see her tracks leading away from the door, following the fresh snow to the horizon.

I went outside after her but then, standing in the new snow in the bright morning, I didn't want to go anywhere. I found an old maple tree and stood beside it, trying to follow the perambulations of the bark. Near the top of the tree was a woodpecker. I moved down the drive, towards the road, counting the inches of my journey.

There are certain things that I wonder about. I wonder what is my destiny. I wonder if there is any frozen orange juice. I wonder if there will be enough wood to last the winter. I wonder how I got here. I like it, but it wasn't part of the plan. But the old plan passes. It is a habit with me, even an affliction. She knows it is in me but she is immune.

On cold days the hydro wires buzz and hum. In the fall they are visible against the sky and remind me of hunting. People like to do their hunting from the back of slowly moving pickup trucks. When they are finished they pile the quail and pheasant into cardboard boxes.

Tonight she is asleep. I am left up to examine my certainties and inspect myself to make sure I am still here.

* * *

We were sitting in a restaurant. Where do you come from? I asked her. I was tracing my lifeline in the salt on the table.

Does it matter?

I come from a river valley. But I didn't say that. I nodded to her comment and pushed the salt onto the floor. River valleys have a way of making you dream about the sea. When I was seven the dream came true, and I lived for a week on an ocean liner. At night there was music but I was asleep. By day I inspected the decks for casualties.

I asked her again where she came from.

Vienna, she said. Until yesterday I lived in Vienna. She twirled a silver ring around a finger. I must have met her in a subway station. Are we both waiting for the same train? was the question she used to approach me. She had been waiting all day for someone like me. She wanted to push me under the train. I took her home with me instead and we spent the night baking a chocolate cake.

I carry her in my wallet now. A picture of a young girl sitting on a bicycle beside her favourite dog. The dog looks puzzled but well fed. Her shoulders are exceptional. They speak of evening gowns and diamond necklaces.

I come from a river valley, I told her. In my apartment is a cedar grove. It used to be hardwood. I took her home with me and we sat in our chairs listening to music and composing sonnets. No matter what I did she still wanted to kill me. I could sense it in the tone of her planned laughs and the way she caressed my arm with her nails.

Why do you want to kill me?

Does it matter?

It did to me. I retain a sense of history: that much is known.

* * *

I want to know everything about you. I want to know how toothpaste tastes in your mouth in the morning, whether your grandfather wore a beard, how far you can swim, whether or not you vote in elections, how it would feel if I kissed your neck, whether you dream in cartoons, which of your thoughts you discard, do you wear perfume?

I want to take you to whatever world we would make together so that we can roll in its snow, compile its grammar, hear its legends told around a campfire on a cool August night. You hate it when I pretend you are inscrutable. You scream that you are flesh and blood; you want children and love and lush Persian rugs. You want to be eaten but won't admit it.

I want to preserve you but don't know how to say it.

There is a pose of a man and a woman standing at a window at dawn looking out with hope at the rising sun. The facts that hope is West and sunrise is East are somehow reconciled. So imagine us, standing in the midst of this cosmic geometry: buying war bonds, raising hamburger, reading the newspaper every day. Is that what it costs to sing in the choir?

While our images go through their motions it is possible for us to slide into each other's bloodstreams. You percolate through my neck into my head and tickle my ears. I blow bubbles out of your breasts and then move down towards your stomach.

We have a mutual friend. Every morning she wakes up and creates the universe. In the summer she plays backyard solitaire. Sometimes I join her. We met there, you and I, by accident. You had promised that you wouldn't come but you distinctly emerged through the hedges and ice cubes. I said you had been stalking me but you just laughed and unfolded yourself to the sun. Would my elbows be grass-stained? Playing cards I mean. I only want you gently. We would never go dancing but we would walk in the snow when the moon was full. Even though they are invisible we are surrounded by guards and fences.

Why do you want me? It matters to me. I retain a sense of history despite everything. I want to know all the details of your suicide.

* * *

I tasted it in the water last night. My friends are murmuring behind closed doors. I am murmuring behind closed doors. But we do not even resist. We stay in bed in the mornings and later go out to join the cows in their soliloquies. We have a cedar grove in our apartment and it is bisected by a stream that flows like a stream running down a mountain. We crouch over it drinking tea and waiting for the trout to spawn.

Like a stream flowing through a cedar grove it has different paths in different seasons. Sometimes it flows under a log bridge and sometimes it steps around it. Other times I pass right through the cedar grove and go to a place carpeted by wild strawberries. We found each other there one day last fall under an oak tree that was too big to cut down.

The first day of spring I drink from the creek in a meaningless ritual that I secretly believe in. We could build a house there, grow bark on our skins, creak in the frost. I didn't used to know that.

For a while we lived in my car. The back trunk was packed with sleeping bags, cooking utensils, two tennis rackets, a box of books, other things I have forgotten. We saw the continental sights, stretching out in our sleeping bags on hardwood floors across the country. Now our friends drop in seasonally. There are times when little happens. The snake has shed his skin they say.

* * *

I can't stop thinking about you. Last night I dreamt we were walking together somewhere, I don't know where. It was a busy city street; the sidewalks were crowded. You were dressed in the black robes of the executioner. You carried the two-headed axe with an absurd ease, as if the blade was not encased in leather. We walked out of the city to a bridge overlooking an empty riverbed. We floated down to the hard-packed sand and you danced for me in the afternoon sun. The light glinted off the edges of your body. You were composed of a million tiny crystals.

I want to know, you said, how to be a better human being.

I nodded and traced your lifeline in the salt.

I want to know, you said, how to be a better human being.

My eyes were filled with your light. There are times when nothing is known: that much is certain. I didn't want you to speak at all. You were supposed to be beyond it. You plied the axe like a yo-yo, slicing me into roasts and chops all boneless so you could have me as a skeleton moving dry and studied through your nights.

In your dreams my eyes burn with prophecies of the apocalypse. Other times you find me as a Tibetan goat. I would never tell you, however, that life is like climbing a mountain blindfolded. It is trite but not enough. Instead I tell you the price of cabbages in New York. I recite my litany of foolish questions and crawl across the foot of your bed licking your knees and purring. You are patient. You hide your disappointment under the pillow and wait for morning. I too am patient. When the time comes we will discuss the news of the war. My body counts have decreased lately and I have never seen your statistics at all. It is the wounded that worry me. I want to make amends but it is hopeless. They have forgiven me already and deposit their duelling scars in the bank.

There will be a second chance, you say. Have you never heard of renewal? I nod sagely and bend my head towards the floor. We have come to each other at a difficult time. Our lives were shedding their unnecessaries. I had already discovered my essential form and was preparing for the final retreat. I had decided to spend the rest of my life in a hammock suspended between the empire state building and my favourite maple tree. My supply lines were well protected and incorruptible. I had a robot trained to go out and do all my work. You will have to admit the plan was at least ingenious.

* * *

We might have been lying side by side. Once I am sure I exist it is no longer necessary. The small of her back fits my hand perfectly. And I know that we were meant for each other. Am I the answer to all your dreams? I ask. She tells me that her dreams were altogether different. I am the answer to the dreams she used to forget. If we were lying down I rolled over so I could look at her directly. The moment is frozen. Within it we exchange a few incidentals: parts of our bodies, some old memories, three postage stamps, a friend that we met on the street, toy soldiers. Afterwards it is as if nothing had happened. We have a cup of tea, I smoke a cigarette, she shuffles the deck and we start all over again. The window is open. It happened in a room.

In the morning it is impossible to know whether I am awake or asleep. She goes about her business and pretends that I live elsewhere. For me it is different. I wake up each day to an obstacle course. There are ablutions to be performed, cogitations on the night before, ingestions of necessaries. One false step will betray the whole day. In the afternoons we play shuffleboard or do the laundry. At night our lives intersect briefly over dinner. But despite the pattern it can happen anytime, even from the most fortified positions. I am a practical man. My walls are covered with charts and equations. I stuff my shoes with old calendars and rolls of film.

* * *

When you came into the garden you were a tortoise disguised as a hare. We recognised each other at once. It had all been predicted. We were supposed to ignite but we circled without moving. We pretended not to notice what was happening. We lay in the grass and watched the sun melt the ice cubes. But it was symbolic of nothing. I have been stalking you for years, peering in your windows and making notes on your habits. When you are nervous you scratch your left elbow. Your face wears a hundred disguises but you think it is always the same. Sometimes, riding streetcars, you find yourself thinking in point form.

When we are together our bodies are awkward. They grow restless wtih maneouvres and delays. And yet they are themselves uncertain. What is expected? What is there to be gained? The chemistry is intricate but not overwhelming. There are easier places. You have a lover who rides a bicycle. He doesn't bore you. It is barely possible that he can swallow a snake.

* * *

I'm not sure if we are suited. You are so fragile. I didn't know that. Sometimes you retreat to cry and count your losses. When I think you are planning your next move you are walking through gardens, looking for a lilac bush or an old man with a bottle of wine. You have a secret scrapbook filled with snapshots of old lovers and the poems they wrote you. You suspect yourself of treason. You are afraid you will rust.

Our bodies have soft spots that have come and gone. We should have met ten years ago. Now it is barely soon enough. What can we do to forget the times we unknowingly walked in and out of each other's lives? We could lie under a willow tree by a river and eat a picnic lunch. If we went wading everything would be changed. Yet you hold back. There is something else you want me to give you first: you are right, we may never meet.

There are other possibilities. You might become a nun. I might fly to the moon. You might say to me one day that you have decided on something else entirely, something completely beyond my understanding. You would say that but wouldn't have anything particular in mind. It would be some sort of hazy fantasy based on a rumour you remember hearing. It is true we are not essential to each other. I could live without you. I would go travelling, or get a job selling vacuum cleaners or do any of the things people do. I am not yet incapacitated. I could dye my hair and get contact lenses. I would probably become a shepherd somewhere. Your fate is less clear. Someone told me you would become a movie star.

We have a mutual friend. Since we met, her mornings have become more complicated. She suspects us of plotting new universes. The other day she was about to ask me directly. She was peeling grapes and onions on her velvet tablecloth.

* * *

We were sitting in a rcstuarant drinking lemonade. Not everyone plays poker, she said. She looked at me across the table. There were no lines about her eyes and her forehead was clear. You might be surprised, she said, at how much you can feel.

We had met somewhere, it must have been the subway station. She had been waiting for me all day with her perfect message. I had come down the stairs to meet her, encased in a red balloon.

I took one of her cigarettes and lit it. She was waiting for me to respond. I could have told her I was from outer space. I could have told her she was from outer space. I took off my balloon and stuck it under the table. She wouldn't care what I said, her job was to deliver the message.

What would you do if I screamed for help?

Just what I am doing, she said, laying four aces between the salt shaker and her coffee cup.

* * *

I think we were riding in the elevator to the top floor of your hotel. It was so many events after the day in the garden that the incident was almost buried in details. Nothing had turned out as predicted. You were slender and taut and instead of moving with diffidence you spring at me out of hidden corners. We grew accustomed to the sight of blood.

What would you do, you said, if someone cut the cables.

I said I didn't know.

What would you do if I told you I never wanted to see

you again?

I don't know, I said. I guess I'd go home and wash the dishes.

You had moved into the hotel room entirely. It was filled with your old trophies and an autographed copy of the confessions of St. Augustine. In the bathroom, hanging from the ceiling, was a burlap bag filled with sand. We had drawn pictures of each other on it in charcoal and periodically added scars and lumps to the faces. There were no pets allowed in the hotel.

We got off the elevator and went into your room. I stood by the door fiddling with the light switch. Shut the light, you said.

Shut it yourself, I said.

Don't be childish, you said. I left the light on and pulled a flashlight from your top dresser drawer.

Tell me the name of your fourth lover.

No.

I poured myself a drink and diluted it with water from your bathroom tap. What would you do, I said, if I told you I never wanted to see you again.

You sat down at your desk calculator and began to press buttons. The machine clicked and whirred. The answer appeared lit up on the dashboard. Nothing, you said, except move out of this hotel room into a hotel down the street.

It was eleven o'clock in the morning. I think we were riding in the elevator to your room in the hotel. In my pockets are stuffed telegrams of condolence that you have been sending me. You are looking at me speculatively. We have finally met. We go to your room and take off all our clothes. We look at each other, surprised. I thought you would be thinner, you say. You look as though you do push-ups in the morning.

Your flesh is different too, I think. You look like a carnivore. You are both softer and firmer than I expected. We feel more encumbered without our clothes than we did with them. I shut the light but we both know what I am doing. And the black velvet curtain is open, leaving a stripe of light across the floor and bed. I wonder what I am waiting for.

* * *

It was difficult at first. We would sit in restaurants holding hands and steal food from supermarkets. But now we are working out a routine. In the mornings you deliver papers while I sleep. In the afternoon I dress up and walk along the street asking for money. When I get home from work dinner is always prepared, hot like it should be. Soon we will want to have children. We are working out a plan to steal a house.

In the meantime I still don't know you. Even the person who is pretending to be you is less than visible. What you do is necessary but not plausible. What have we given up for each other? What is the meaning of our time together? I thought we had recognized each other. I used to peer in your windows and take notes. Now I am not so sure. You claim that you are human. Very well: I will be human too. Perhaps it is not so easy. Tomorrow you could kidnap a psychiatrist.

The fact is that I fell into your handbag by mistake. I was on my way somewhere else. I was on my way to a subway station to meet a friend. She wants to push me under a train but she won't. We will sit in a restaurant and tell each other stories. She will stroke my knees and take me back to her apartment. We will lie on her bed and make love without thinking about it. We will go for a walk in a forest. We will eat oranges in the morning.

* * *

We come to each other at different times of the day and night. Sometimes she sleeps curled around me, her hand tracing patterns on my chest and stomach. Sometimes we call each other by different names.

There is much that is unknown with us. We scatter it about the house and take it for walks. Everything is permitted its own existence. We drink tea in our cedar grove and follow the stream up the mountain. Our moments are bracketed, sometimes unaware of each other. There are nights when I see your shadow at the window. I found footprints in the garden once last summer.

You left me a note under a strawberry plant and I sent you flowers at Easter.

She hasn't seen you yet but she suspects it is herself. We co-exist. We are covered with bits of each other's flesh. We come to each other at different times of the day and night seeking ourselves. Contracts are torn up and renewed. Sometimes we make love unknown to each other. My arms are undecided. There are times when she senses my destiny. I want to ask her what it is but she is immune to my questions. She paints watercolours in the garden and dreams of chocolate pie and children. We stalk the hedges planning tunnels here and stonework there.

She sees herself moving through the field, the grass brushing her knees. She listens to the stories of the cedar grove and kneels at the stream for water. When she rises the tips of her hair are wet and as she walks she swings it about her head, pretending that she is a cloud, that she is beginning to drift.

We leave each other signs of our comings and goings. At times she is morose.

* * *

Some things are known. That much is certain. I know, for example, that if I ask you, you will say you love me. Contracts are torn up and renewed. You have often intimated other fates. It is possible that we may meet.

AFTER DINNER BUTTERFLIES

They were sitting in the library, drinking coffee. She noticed that he had a hand in one of his pockets, he seemed to be fiddling with something.

George?

What?

What have you go there?

Nothing, he said.

Show it to me immediately.

It's nothing, he said. He took his hand out of his pocket and puffed elaborately on his cigar. Good cigar, he said.

No cigar, she said. Take that thing out of your pocket.

George stood up and leaned against the mantle, still puffing on his cigar. He pulled a rabbit out of a vase. Look at the nice rabbit, he said.

Put it away.

He stuck the rabbit out the window and returned to his chair. He picked up an old newspaper and started reading it. When he was sure she wasn't looking he put his hand back into his pocket.

George!

What?

Let me see it.

There's nothing here.

Oh yes there is. I saw you fiddling with it. Now let me see it.

Alright, he said. He reached into his pocket. Then he changed his mind. No, you have to guess.

I'm not playing one of your stupid games.

Okay, George said. Let's forget it then. He re-lit his cigar and stuck his hand back in his pocket. Time passed. His cigar went out. Mary got another cup of coffee. The fire was going. George kept his hand in his pocket. He got tired of of the newspaper. He went over to the library table and sat down to work on the jig-saw puzzle. He was so absorbed in a little bit of orange and green that he didn't hear Mary sneak up on him.

There, she exclaimed. I've got it. Her hand was in his

pocket. Then she withdrew it, puzzled. There's nothing there, she said.

They sat back down. A few moments later she noticed that George was working his hand in his pocket. When he looked up he saw her watching him. Do you want to see what's in my pocket?

You don't have anything in your pocket.

Yes I do.

Prove it.

Okay, George said. He reached into his pocket and pulled out a shiny bit of metal. It appeared to be some sort of complicated miniature. He brought it over to her, holding it cupped in the palm of his hand. But when she reached for it, he drew back. Don't touch, he said. You'll break it. He held it out to her again so she could look at it. It was a metal sphere with little red things sticking out of its silver surface.

What is it? she asked.

It's a space ship.

That's nice.

Watch this. He walked to the side of the room farthest from the fire. Come here, he said. She stood beside him. He threw his metal gizmo into the fire. There was a clicking sound, metal against brickwork.

Well, she said, you could have done that with a firecracker.

Right, George said. They sat back down. After a while Mary noticed that she had, in a very faint way, the same sort of feeling in her stomach that she sometimes got in an elevator.

George, she said.

Yes?

I feel funny. I feel like we're in an elevator.

Or in a spaceship, George said. He walked over to the sideboard and poured himself a glass of sherry. Cheers, he said.

Don't think you can upset me with your silly games.

Oh no, George said.

I was once married to a Hungarian Count.

Were there bagpipes at your wedding? Yes there were. I was there. I remember them clearly: they were off key.

Mary crossed her legs and tried to pull her skirt down over her knees. They felt strange, as if something was about to land on them. George, she said, prove to me that we are on a spaceship.

Alright, George said. He snapped his fingers. Nothing happened. Then a delicate golden butterfly landed on Mary's right knee. Isn't that beautiful?

Isn't what beautiful? Mary said. She could have sworn that a golden butterfly had landed on her knee.

The music, George said. He turned up the radio so that the library was filled with sounds. A second golden butterfly landed on Mary's knee.

I don't like it, she said. She got up and turned the radio off. The butterflies followed her, circling her head like a halo. Go on, she said when she sat down, flicking at her shoulders, go sit on someone else. But they just came back.

You'd better leave them alone, George said.

Why? I don't like them.

But they like you.

I don't like the feeling of them sitting on my shoulders, watching me.

They're very pretty.

I can't even see them without straining my neck.

I'll get you a mirror, George said.

I don't want a mirror. Let's just forget them and see if they go away.

Alright, George said. He lit a new cigar and sipped at his sherry. After a while Mary noticed that he had a hand in his pocket again and seemed to be fiddling with something.

George.

What?

What are you doing now?

Nothing, George said. He took his hand out of his pocket. I'm just trying to get this damned thing turned around.

What thing?

The spaceship.

The butterflies were still perched on Mary's shoulders, waiting patiently. George snapped his fingers again. A white wolf appeared in the middle of the room. Its eyes were as golden as butterflies. It walked over to George's chair, climbed up into it, and licked its paws. Go on, George said. Sit on the floor. The wolf looked up at him and then returned to its paws.

You see? You don't know how to do anything right.

I'm sorry, George said.

What a lovely wolf. Look at its eyes.

I wish it would get off my chair.

It likes you, Mary said. That's why it wants to sit on your chair.

If it really liked me it would get off of my chair and fetch a stick or something. He took a cigar from the mantle and waved it in the air. Fetch, doggie, he said. He threw the cigar across the room. The wolf looked at him, looked over at the cigar, raised its eyebrows, and went back to sleep.

That reminds me, Mary said. Did I ever tell you that I was once married to a Hungarian Count?

Yes, George said. You just told me five minutes ago. Do you mind if I sit on the arm of your chair? The butterflies were still perched on her shoulders, waiting patiently.

Yes, she said. I do mind. Why don't you stand at the mantle and try to look unconcerned?

There was a knock at the door. Come in, George shouted. A man wearing grey coveralls and carrying a toolbox entered the room.

Is this the place with the television?

Yes, George said, it's there in the corner. I don't know what's wrong with it.

Probably blew a tube, the repairman said. It often happens. Nice dog.

Yes.

The repairman pushed the television out from the wall and began poking at its innards.

Do you want a glass of sherry?

No thanks, the man said. He reached into the television and pulled out three stuffed camels. Here's your problem, he said. There were three stuffed camels in the back of your television set.

Oh, George said. I was hiding them there for my wife's birthday.

You should've told me. He turned on the set. Works fine now. He pushed the television back against the wall and packed up his tools. I'll send you a bill, he said, and left the room.

The repairman made two more housecalls and then went home. His wife was sitting up, waiting for him. He changed out of his coveralls, washed up, and then got his dinner out of the oven and a beer from the refrigerator.

How did it go tonight?

The usual. Is Jimmy asleep?

Yes, he went to bed hours ago.

What else did you do?

Nothing much, she said. She crossed her legs and tried to pull her skirt down over her knees. I watched TV for a while and read Jimmy a story.

Is there anything for dessert?

There's some pie. He went into the kitchen and found a coconut cream pie in the refrigerator. He brought it back into the living room.

Have you ever wanted to throw a pie in my face?

Once, she said. Remember that dance we went to just after we started going out? You put an ice cube down my dress? Well, when you took me home my parents were still up and we had strawberry pie with whipped cream. You were all sitting at the table and I was getting the pie. I could feel the ice water trickling down my skin and the inside of my dress was wet. I almost dumped the pie right on your head.

He leaned back and lit a cigarette. God, he said, that

must have been ten years ago.

Eleven, she said. Eleven years and two months. I remember standing there. I was just about to turn the pie onto your head when I decided to marry you. She crossed the room and sat down beside him on the couch. I don't know why I never told you, she said. I always meant to.

What else didn't you ever tell me?

Did I ever tell you that I was once married to a Hungarian Count?

No, he said. And I wouldn't believe you if you did. He was leaning back with his eyes closed. She dipped her hand into the pie and spread it gently over his face. She formed little ridges at the eyebrows, being careful not to get any into his eyes. She spread it on his cheeks with the palms of her hands and then swirled it with her index finger so that his cheeks stood out in spiral puffs. She gave him a moustache and a beard – a nice pointed van dyke beard that reminded her of a picture. When the beard started to drip she pushed it back up onto his chin and drew a picture of a rose in it. All the whipped cream was gone. She took a fork and fed him some of the coconut filling.

How does it taste?

Good, he said.

I should have saved you some of the whipped cream.

That's alright. He stuck out his tongue and licked a path along his right cheek. Tonight I saw a woman with two golden butterflies perched on her shoulders.

That's nice dear.

THE EMPTY ROOM

The author sat in his study. It was a dull grey day. His floor was littered with the crumpled-up remnants of unwritten novels. His desk was entirely clean except for his typewriter and a fresh sheet of paper. He lit a cigarette. He cleaned his nails. He inspected the wallpaper.

She was wearing a khaki shirt, her hair bleached blond by the sun fell long and free past her shoulders, swung free in the still heat, moved slowly across the desert against the background of movie cameras and tired people, settled and splashed across his pillow, wrapped him up and then spun him out like a washed-out top, spinning across the desert nights like a bright paper streamer that had mistaken a press conference for a New Year's Eve party, that everyone pretended not to see or notice but constantly found winding and unwinding in their plastic coffee cups filled with scotch and tepid water. She was wearing a khaki shirt, her hair bleached blond and free, swinging her head gently back and forth, her hair slapping his face drawing pink flushes out of his cheeks splashing the colour against the walls of the tent, spinning out the desert night.

I need you, he said. She was wearing the shirt open, making a tent around him, slowly brushing her breasts back and forth across his eyelids. He had come unwillingly, disturbed his schedule, been prepared to be quarrelsome and brief. They had flown him from Toronto to London. From London to Morocco. A car had picked him up and driven him to a village. There he had been met by the girl, in an open jeep. He had sat beside her while she drove, sullen and unused to the sun and the heat. He felt middle-aged and distended. He was smoking himself to death. The long succession of parties had stupefied him, he was blocked on a novel about a lampshade, someone had decided he could fix the script. It was a film about a man and a woman who are dropped by parachute into a desert by mistake. It turns out that they knew each other in public school. They recount their lives to each other while trying to invent water. Despite everything they fall in love. She gets pregnant. He hunts for armadillos by night; she pounds cactus seeds into bread while he sleeps.

He sucked her ear lobe. I've got it, he said. They are rescued by a helicopter. While flying back to civilization she delivers the baby aloft. But when they get back to the city they discover they are not meant for one another after all. The last scene takes place in a sandbox and the movie ends with the image of a bucket of sand, emptying remorselessly into the sunset.

This is better, he said. They are out in the desert doing what they are doing. Meanwhile there is a political crisis. Atomic war follows. Streams of refugees converge on them, in this last place safe from radiation. They build a new world. He has an affair with a Portugese seamstress. She says she will not forgive him but just as the baby is being born she does. The movie ends with the face of the baby emerging from the woman; gradually the face is defined. It is Hope. The background dissolves into a mushroom cloud but at the same time the face grows until finally it fills the whole screen. It becomes translucent and there is behind it the image of the man and woman kissing, tears streaking down their faces. The tears turn into a river, flow into the sea, there is music. . .

They were driving in the open jeep. Have a drink if you like, she said, pointing to the glove compartment. He opened it and saw, nestled among the maps and crushed-up cigarette packages, a revolver.

It's for snakes, she said. Don't worry, we haven't seen one yet. My mother made me promise to take it.

What am I doing here?

I don't know, she said. I thought you were supposed to be the guy that wrote the novel.

Yes, but they've made quite a few changes. The novel was set in Edmonton.

Oh.

They are crawling on their hands and knees, he said. The sun is burning down on them. Their skin is wrinkled dry and their fingers grip the desert like claws. They see ahead of them the mirage of an old Hollywood movie set, a cowboy town of the early nineteenth century. But it is not a mirage. As they come closer they see the dusty buildings. Men are lounging against the rails chewing tobacco and playing cards. Women ride up and down the streets in buckboard wagons. They go into a hotel and register. It is their first time together. He undresses and lies down on the bed.

She is wearing a khaki shirt. She sits astride him, her shirt open, making a tent about his face, nodding her head slowly so that her hair caresses his face, draws the colour out of him and splashes it against the walls of the tent, spins him out into the desert night like a firefly parade.

I need you, he said. But I wouldn't die without you.

The author sat in his study. He thought he might write a novel about a diplomat who lived in a sauna. He put a new piece of paper in his typewriter. He cleaned his nails. The telephone rang; it was his dentist.

I know, he said.

It won't work, she said. They were at the bottom of a well, up to their waists in wet sand. Here, she said. We'll play X's and O's.

We're sinking.

Goodbye, she said. She put her arms around him and dismantled his spine.

They find they are standing in an old bucket. They rip off their clothes into long strips and braid them together into a rope. Straining heroically, they pull themselves up. When they get to the surface they see they are surrounded by an immense colony of army ants. The ants move towards them, working their mandibles suggestively. They lower themselves back into the well but the ants begin to pour down the sides. They raise themselves part way up but the ants, piling into a red mound, gradually fill the well. They are forced to the surface again. There are still millions of ants there, crowded about the lip of the well. There is no possibility of escape. A

World War Two tank is heading towards them at a hundred miles an hour. It is beginning to rain. The temperature falls. In the distance bombs are going off. They are standing in the bucket, the ants are chewing through their clothing and hair. She screams.

And then?

Fast cut to a restaurant in Paris. They are sitting eating frogs' legs an an outdoor café. He is pouring champagne. She lifts the glass to her lips and opens her mouth. An army of red ants emerge, endless streams of them. They cover the table, they move onto the sidewalk, they devour all of Paris. They find the Eiffel Tower and climb all over it. At the last moment, when it is all ants and no tower, it crumbles.

They were driving in the jeep over the open desert. She reached into the glove compartment and took out her revolver. She put it into her mouth and pulled the trigger.

I thought you said it was loaded.

I thought it was. She put the revolver back and stopped the car. She got out of the car and slammed the door behind her. I think I'll walk, she said, and started hopping across the desert on one foot.

He moved his nose along her belly until it buried itself in her sternum. It might have been the twelfth night: they could have been lying in his tent, licking their wounds and making little growling sounds. I have a cat at home, she said. It likes to lie on the table and wrap its tail around the candle-sticks.

The author sat in his study. He had given up on his memoirs. He thought he might write a novel about a wastepaper basket. His wife brought him a cup of coffee. Thank you, he said.

Don't forget my mother's coming to dinner tonight. How's the work going?

He stood up and stretched. Terrible. He put his arms around his wife. He nibbled at her ear lobe. Her hair was set in tight iron curlers.

Don't, she said. You know I have to wash the floor. He sat back down at his desk and waited until she had closed the door. He lit a cigarette and sipped at his coffee.

He didn't die without her: he forgot her slowly. He went back to the desert and set up a nightclub in an oasis. It had red and blue neon lights. He would stand by the swimming pool at night smoking cigarettes and gazing intractably at the horizon. Occasionally he would allow himself a beautiful woman. But he was faithful to her in his own way.

I waited for you, he said. They were standing at the edge of the desert. Her hair, bleached blond by the sun, fell long and free past her shoulders, swung free in the desert night. They walked out into the sand, away from the lights and noise. They found a place and he spread out his coat so they could sit down.

I waited for you, he said. She let the words fall out of his mouth. She didn't say anything. Her fingers were long and tapered. She asked him for a cigarette. He looked across at her. She unbuttoned her blouse and made a tent around them. She didn't say anything. They could hear the sounds of music moving faintly across the sand and wind. His skin was tanned and hardened from his years in the desert. Her nails traced rivers of blood on his body.

I'm late for supper, she said.

So am I. The movie ended as it had begun. They were driving across the desert in her jeep.

Have a drink if you like, she said. He opened the glove compartment and saw a revolver nestled among the maps. Don't worry, she said. It's just there.

Her mother talked in the candlelight. She had long tapered fingers, lacquered nails. I hear you're working on another novel, she said.

Yes. He looked over to his wife. She was already watching him, waiting, her eyes warning him.

It must be so interesting to write. I mean, where does it all come from? Do you just make it up?

Yes, he said. I try to.

You must have someone who inspires you. She wrapped her fingers around the salt shaker. These really are beautiful, she said. Where did you get them?

They were a wedding present, his wife said. She moved the wine away from him. She kicked him under the table.

It's a beautiful day today, he said. I went for a walk.

Yes, his wife said, I love spring. It's the best season.

We're having the rock garden done over, her mother said. It's a pity you don't have a bigger yard. She tapped her nails on the wineglass. What a delicious salad. Where did you get the lettuce?

A little boy sold it to me, he said. I found him in the cucumber patch.

The two women laughed. That's very funny, his wife said. Her mother coughed.

Did I tell you that I'm going to Spain this summer?

Really?

Yes. As soon as the garden's done. I love Spain. It's so romantic. She paused and looked at her watch. We'd better not be late. Are you sure you won't come?

You know how he is when he's working, his wife said. She came into his study before they left. He stood up and put his arms around her. Don't, she said. I have to go. But later.

He didn't die without her: he forgot her slowly. He went to the garage and got a can of kerosene. He brought it into the house and sprinkled it liberally in the centre hall. He went to the living room and doused the drapes with it. He made a little trail that led from the front door to the drapes. He went to his study and poured the remains on his typewriter. Then he returned to the front door and lit the kerosene.

What are you doing?

I used to be a magician but I wasn't very good.

And?

I don't know. I thought I should do something useful.

And?

That's all. She was sitting astride him, leaning forward and combing his scalp with her breath. I've got it, he said. They are crawling through the desert, remembering a spelling contest. I love you, he shouts, through his cracked lips. Music starts up. They are back in the classroom. It is decorated like a church and the teacher performs the wedding ceremony. Afterwards they are driving through the desert in her open jeep. She is much younger than he is. Her throat is smooth and brown. He expects nothing from her.

And?

That's all. They had found an oasis and he was lying on his back with his eyes closed. She said nothing. He was listening to the palm leaves. The water lapped gently on the shore. Her hair, bleached blond by the sun, formed a tent around them. She was sitting astride him, leaning forward and combing his scalp with her breath.

TOO BAD GALAHAD

TOO BAD GALAHAD

Galahad was a knight of the Round Table. This is how he died.

*

Galahad was the perfect knight. He spent his life in search of the Holy Grail. When he died he found it. It happened at the last possible moment. Just as he was losing consciousness an angel appeared to him and said: Galahad, one more thing.

What is it?

The angel whipped out a silver necklace and slipped it around Galahad's neck. There, said the angel, now you have it.

Thank God, said Galahad. I never knew it would happen this way.

*

The Holy Grail wasn't really a necklace. It was a silver chalice. The chalice wasn't really silver. It was a bunch of molecules and atoms cleverly arranged by God to look exactly like silver in the bright light but to be invisible in the dark.

This is how Galahad received the silver chalice which really wasn't silver but was the Holy Grail.

Galahad was employed as a master of English in a small private school in the English countryside. He lived in a thatch-roofed stone cottage near the school. Around the house were gardens and arbours, trees and vines. Galahad grew all his own vegetables and only took lunches at the school.

One day the headmaster sent for Galahad.

Galahad, he said. I hear you have been teaching the pupils that you are the second incarnation of the good knight Galahad and that instead of giving them lessons you have been indoctrinating them into the rituals of the Round Table.

Yes sir, said Galahad. Galahad was always perfectly honest. Why have you been doing this, Galahad?

The truth is, sir, that I am unacquainted with grammar but knowledgable about morality. I have done my duty.

Very well, Galahad. You have two alternatives. Either you apologise and reform your ways or you will be released from your position.

I cannot apologise, sir, for I have done no wrong.

That is all,Galahad.

Galahad left the headmaster's office and went home to his little stone cottage. That evening all his pupils came to wish their master well in his next life. A pitcher of hemlock juice was prepared. Galahad set them all upon his knee and discoursed on the meaning of death.

When it was midnight they left him. At five minutes after midnight Galahad emptied the pitcher of hemlock. He had three minutes to live. Part way through the second minute the pitcher turned into the silver chalice. When the lights went out it became invisible and Galahad was dead.

*

Galahad's mother was Elaine and his father was Lancelot. Galahad was the perfect knight but Lancelot was the most heroic. He was King Arthur's right hand man and dabbled with Guenevere, Arthur's queen but Lancelot's passion. Perhaps Galahad's virtue was a compensation for Lancelot's indiscretion. Arthur never found out about Lancelot and Guenevere.

Lancelot and Guenevere used to pick daisies together in the fields surrounding Camelot. When King Arthur was away they spent the nights in Guenevere's room. All this was before Elaine.

Elaine was young and beautiful. She was the daughter of King Pelles. Lancelot won her in a tournament and carried her off from her castle into a legend. When he took off his helmet she was horrified to find that he was older than she had imagined. After they dismounted she noticed that he was also quite short. About five feet tall. But there was only one horse so she made the best of things.

Galahad was the perfect knight. He devoted his life to the search for the Holy Grail. It was a good life and it helped to know what he was searching for. But he didn't know where to look. On one of his journeys he encountered a dragon. He drew out his sword to cut off its head.

With this sword I slay thee, said Galahad and swept it into the dragon's neck.

But the sword bounced off the dragon and Galahad lost his balance.

With this gulp I swallow thee, said the dragon. It shot out its forked tongue and swallowed Galahad whole. Then it turned into a whale and swam out to sea. Then Galahad tickled the whale's stomach until it had to vomit him up. Then Galahad began to drown.

As he was sinking for the third time he clutched at the last straw. It turned out to be the Holy Grail and he died happy.

Galahad was the perfect knight. He was to the Round Table as St. Paul was to Jesus. He was so perfect that he was a prig. No one liked Galahad but they all admired him. Being perfect, Galahad didn't even have the vanity to fortify himself by recognising that it was his perfection that caused him to be unpopular. He tried to swear and kill and wench with the rest of the knights but he could never really get into it. No matter what it was he couldn't quite do it because at the very moment he was about to he would think, maybe if I do this I won't get the Holy Grail and my whole life will be meaningless. Galahad was thus the inventor of Coitus Interruptus.

One night, while practicing punctuation with his girlfriend Georgina, Galahad blew it. As it happened he was so mortified that he died. That is how Galahad found the Holy Grail.

Georgina was so pleased it took her two hours to realise he was dead. When she did she rolled over and lit a candle. Galahad was covered with tiny silver drops. Then, right before her eyes, the silver drops began to evaporate.When they were all gone so was Galahad. Georgina was so surprised and scared she didn't dare tell anyone. She said Galahad had gone off to the Holy Land in search of the Holy Grail. Everyone has believed her to this day.

When Galahad realised he was dying he felt relieved. Thank God it's all over, he thought. I've spent my whole life searching for the Holy Grail and I've never known where to look. I've been the perfect knight and it hasn't helped. My mother was beautiful and my father was brave but I never had a chance because I never knew where to look. All my life I believed I would find the Holy Grail and then I could be like everyone else but now that I'm dying I'm glad it's over.

Galahad closed his eyes and saw a choir of seraphim singing Christmas carols. They were dressed in golden robes and had halos. He couldn't make out the tune.

One angel out of the many came forward to Galahad and bowed. Greetings, Galahad, it said. You have been perfect all your life. Perfection is its own reward. Congratulations.

Just a moment, Galahad said. What about the Holy Grail?

Oh yes, said the seraph. We've got a million of them here. Help yourself.

*

One day Gálahad was riding through the forest when he came upon an evil knight dressed in black armour.

Stop, said the evil knight. You money or your life.

I have no money, said Galahad, and I'm using my life to search for the Holy Grail.

The evil knight grasped his lance and held it high in the air. Alright, he said. I know who you are. You are the perfect knight Galahad. What a joke. You never have any fun at all and everyone laughs at you behind your back. You think you're so perfect. But really you're just a fraud. Don't you know there's no Holy Grail? I bet you're too weak to fight. If you want to search for the Holy Grail you'll have to get past me.

I'm sorry, Galahad said, but I don't joust with strangers.

Then prepare to die, said the black knight as he bore down on Galahad.

Galahad crooked his lance in his arm and charged. The black knight was coming towards him. He was going towards the black knight. They crashed. Both Galahad and the evil stranger were knocked off their horses.

Well, said the evil knight, dusting off his chain mail seat, you're not such a sissy as I thought. But you still haven't escaped me. With that he pulled out a huge black sword.

Just a moment, Galahad said. I'll only fight you if you lift your visor.

The evil knight lifted his visor. It was King Arthur. Sorry, boy, said the King. Things get to be a bore around the castle. Promise not to tell anyone and I'll let you go.

Galahad was the perfect knight. Once a month he stayed up all night praying in the main chapel. The chapel had stained glass windows and a stone floor. Galahad would pray kneeling in the middle of the centre aisle on the night of the full moon. The moon filled the room with shadows and covered the floor with colours from the windows. The floor was stones with mortar in between the stones and as the moon moved across the sky the stones and mortar took on different colours and brightnesses. When he got tired of praying he would crawl around the chapel following the mortared veins of the floor with his fingers. It never led him to the Holy Grail but it kept him awake and he always felt good the next day.

When he died Galahad imagined he was lying on his back on the floor of the chapel and that the Holy Grail was the shaft of moonlight that came through the windows right to his face.

He imagined that he travelled up the shaft of moonlight to the moon where everything was perfectly silver and chaste and he knew that he would sit on the moon for all eternity circling round the earth and sending messages to knights praying in the chapel.

The astronauts went to the moon to look for Galahad but they won't find him. He has turned into a pillar of salt and makes notes on their progress.

Guenevere loved Galahad as if he were her own son. Sometimes she wished things had turned out that way even though she liked being a Queen and thought Arthur was okay.

When Galahad was little, Guenevere went out of her way to befriend Elaine and spend time with Galahad. Elaine loved Guenevere but felt uncomfortable with her. She didn't like the way Guenevere looked at Arthur, which was without sufficient devotion, or the way Lancelot looked at Guenevere, which was with too much familiarity. Elaine could have figured out the reason for all this but she had very little imagination. She preferred to keep her soul clean and concentrate on raising Galahad to be a knight worthy of the Round Table.

After Galahad was born Lancelot was not attentive to Elaine. He was courteous and performed his duties towards her but he was not attentive. Elaine was unhappy.

Despite the fact that she didn't trust Guenevere she decided to confide in her. There was no-one else to confide in.

Guenevere was secretly happy that Lancelot had remained true to their memory but also thought that Lancelot should love this sweet young princess who had been carried away from her castle to live in a legend. She heard Elaine out and then, the next afternoon, summoned Lancelot to her room.

Lancelot, she said. Your wife is unhappy. Soon she will be miserable.

Alright, Lancelot said, I'll do what I can. He picked up a dozen roses for Elaine and brought them to her.

He hired a babysitter for a week and took her on a tour of the countryside. He made love to her late at night and smiled at her in the morning. He even started brushing his teeth.

That is how Galahad remembered Lancelot. Standing outside their door brushing his teeth with a twig and spitting blood onto the ground.

The English have always had problems with their teeth.

When Galahad died he lost control of his mind. He tried to remember the Ten Commandments but he couldn't. He tried to pray but he found himself reciting nursery rhymes. He tried to picture Arthur and Guenevere sitting on their thrones but instead he had an image of Arthur stroking the knee of a young servant girl. He tried to remember his mother but he only remembered his house. When he gave up on sorting out his past and let his mind go blank it filled up with memories of lives he hadn't lived. He had heard that his life should flash before his eyes; instead of that the Holy Grail flashed before his eyes. The Holy Grail was a huge goat covered with red fur. Greetings, it said. I am the Holy Grail.

Wow, said Galahad. No wonder I could never find you.

Well, said the goat, it's alright now. Hop on and I'll give you a ride to heaven.

Wow, said Galahad. You mean I get to go to heaven? Even though I never found the Holy Grail?

Of course you do, said the red goat. Everyone goes to heaven. Didn't anyone ever tell you that?

No, said Galahad, but I wish someone had.

It doesn't matter, said the goat. To tell the truth it's a lie.

*

Merlin the magician was a magician and carpenter who made the Round Table. He made it with an axe and a hammer and didn't use any nails at all. This was not his only magical feat but is one of his best ones and has been copied by carpenters many times.

Around the Round Table sat the Knights of the Round Table. Nobody knows what they did there. Probably they ate and drank and bragged.

Galahad was a Knight of the Round Table. His task was to find the Holy Grail. Percival before him had also had this task but it was too much for him. He passed it on to Galahad.

King Arthur got the Round Table for a wedding present when he married Guenevere. It was there that Galahad died. He died of humiliation at the Round Table when someone teased him about not finding the Holy Grail. As he was dying he slipped from his chair.

As he slipped from his chair he fell to the floor. It was there that he found the Holy Grail. It had been under the table the whole time and he could have found it years ago.

When they picked him up from the floor Galahad had shrunk to one fiftieth of his usual size and was curled up in the foetal position inside the Holy Grail.

They set him on the mantelpiece as an example for young knights.

Much has been said about Merlin the magician but little has been said about his dunce cap with stars on it. The dunce cap with stars on it is the Holy Grail.

The Holy Grail was supposed to be the cup which Jesus used at the Last Supper and which held his blood after the Crucifixion.

One day when Jesus was alone in the desert battling temptations he ran into an old man trying to build a round table without any nails. What's this? Jesus asked. Why are you building a round table? Have you ever seen a round room?

There are those who have eyes yet do not see, muttered the old man.

Say, said Jesus, that's a pretty good line. Mind if I use it?

Jesus and the old man stood in the empty desert while the old man worked on his table. That's a pretty nice table, Jesus said.

Yes, said the carpenter. Would you like to have it?

No thanks. But I like your hat.

It's yours, said Merlin. He took off his duncecap and put it on Jesus's head. There, he said. It looks a lot better on you than it did on me anyway.

The hat was Jesus's lucky charm. He wore it to the Last Supper and drank from it. He wore it to the Crucifixion too but it was invisible so no one noticed it. Merlin's hat was the Holy Grail.

One day Galahad asked Merlin if he knew where the Holy Grail was. Sure, Merlin said. But I can't tell you.

Galahad and Merlin were sitting on the edge of the legend spending a quiet afternoon talking.

Well, said Galahad, how am I supposed to find it if you won't help me?

I'll give you a hint, Merlin said. No matter where you look it won't help but no matter where you look you're bound to find it.

Aha, said Galahad. Then it must be right here. He was so

excited that he fell off the legend into a footnote. As he fell Merlin threw the hat after him. That is how Galahad died and that is how Galahad found the Holy Grail.

Merlin made himself another duncecap and no one ever knew the difference.

*

Georgina loved Galahad but Galahad didn't love Georgina. At least not the way Georgina wanted to be loved.

Galahad loved Georgina with his purity. He wrote verses to her in iambic pentameter and brought her white lilies by the dozen.

Georgina loved Galahad for his body. She found his purity a bore. Galahad had a very nice body. It was straight and muscular and looked good under all that chain mail. His face had saxon features and his hair was long and blond and parted in the middle. Beneath his well-formed eyebrows were irridescent blue eyes and dark curling eyelashes. He used to like to look at his reflection in the water.

One day while he was leaning over a pond gazing at his irridescent blue eyes Georgina snuck up behind him and leaned over.

She waited until the reflection of her lips was next to the reflection of his lips. Then she gave him a big kiss.

Galahad was so surprised that he fell into the pond.

Georgina thought he looked so funny thrashing about in the water with his armour on that she took off all her clothes and jumped in after him.

But that is not how Galahad died.

*

One day, Arthur asked Lancelot to undertake the quest for the Holy Grail. It would be just the thing, he said, to put some life into the order of the Round Table. Everything here is getting old and decadent. Something new and noble has to happen. Something that will give everyone the feeling that what we are doing is in the present and not the past.

Lancelot agreed it was a fine idea. But why not let one of the younger knights do it, he said. I've done so much already. I'm too old and too lazy. It was the only time Lancelot ever refused Arthur.

Thus finally Galahad was chosen to take on the Holy Quest. He, like Arthur, pulled the sword from a granite rock. When Lancelot heard it was his son who was chosen he sighed but didn't say anything.

Galahad found the Holy Grail. He died clutching it. In that last moment of consciousness he realised he had lived his whole life in order to die finding the Holy Grail. Oh well, he thought, Georgina has grown old and ugly and I've been hiding a paunch under my armour. I never would have enjoyed retirement.

They buried him in a field outside the castle and planted buttercups on his grave. Those who wept, wept, but everyone else was happy that it was finally over.

This is how Galahad was chosen to lead the search for the Holy Grail.

There was a seat at the Round Table at which no-one dared sit. Those who had tried to sit in it were struck dead immediately.

One day the following gold letters appeared on the table: *Four hundred winters and fifty four accomplished after the passion of our Lord Jesus Christ ought this siege to be fulfilled.*

On that day Galahad, son of Lancelot, first appeared at Camelot. He walked up to the Round Table and sat in the forbidden seat. He looked young and perfect and everyone was surprised that he wasn't struck dead.

Don't all sit there staring at me, he said. Pass me some supper.

Many choose but few are chosen.

*

Galahad was employed as a master of English in a small private school in the countryside. He lived in a thatch-roofed stone cottage near the school. Around the house were gardens and arbours, trees and vines. Galahad grew all his own vegetables and only took lunches at the school.

The name of the headmaster of the school was Merlin. One day Merlin sent for Galahad.

When Galahad was seated in his office Merlin took off his hat. He pulled out a few rabbits and a dozen handkerchiefs and then leaned back in his chair.

Galahad, you are the perfect teacher.

Thank you sir, even though I am not perfect.

Never mind, Merlin said. I have a job for you.

What's that?

I want you to take the year off and find the Holy Grail. The members of your English class will accompany you. It will be an educational experience. It is the newest thing in progressive education.

Right sir, said Galahad. We'll leave this afternoon.

At the end of the year Galahad reported back to the headmaster. Did you find it? Merlin asked.

No sir.

Well then, Galahad, how do you propose to assign marks?

I've given them all an essay to write called The Search for the Holy Grail.

Very good, Merlin said. Bring the essays to me when they are done.

A week later Galahad brought Merlin a stack of essays. Merlin leafed through them and made them disappear into his hat.

Then he rattled his hat until a silver chalice came out. Galahad, this is the Holy Grail.

Galahad took the chalice from Merlin and examined it. It was exceedingly bright and shiny. A ray of sunlight reflected from the Grail into his right eye and killed him. Merlin stuffed Galahad and the chalice into his hat. He put the hat on his head and buzzed for his secretary.

Georgina, he said, Galahad has gone to heaven. Post a notice on the bulletin board and cancel English classes for the day.

Very well sir, said Georgina.

When Galahad got to the moon he spent his first few years just sitting on his throne and watching the earth. But after a while he got bored with that and decided to seek adventure. He walked around and whistled for his horse Silver. Silver came out from behind a rock. He was wearing a saddle and had all of Galahad's knightly costumes and weapons draped over him. Galahad put them on and mounted Silver.

Since he was dead Galahad didn't have to sleep and besides the moon is not very big. So he was confident that he could explore it all. But appearances are deceiving. He found it too hot on the sunny side of the moon and had to ride carefully along the edge of the shadow. After riding for a few days he came to a grove of stalagmites. There, in the midst of the grove, attended by three elves playing flutes, lay Sir Lancelot.

Galahad and Lancelot were very glad to see each other and embraced warmly. They told each other everything that had happened since they had last seen each other and then decided to go looking for other knights. Soon all the knights of the Round Table were found and re-united.

But there were no women to be found on the moon. This caused a great problem because with no women there was no one for whom to do great deeds and no colours to wear in a jousting tournament.

So the knights began quarrelling with one another. But a strange thing happened. Whenever one knight struck another knight they both were instantly and permanently evaporated.

When the company was down to half its original size there was a meeting. All agreed that there should be no more fighting. But soon quarrelling broke out again.

The knights decided that since they couldn't live peacefully they might as well go out in style. They organised a tournament and drew lots to see who would go first. As each pair of knights clashed they would evaporate. Their horses evaporated too. Finally only Galahad and Lancelot were left.

Galahad addressed Lancelot. Lancelot, he said, I am willing to evaporate but I admire you too much to make you disappear. You are the bravest knight of all and my own Father. I will strike myself and you will be the last knight. Having spoken thus Galahad plunged his sword into his own heart. But nothing happened because he was dead already.

Look, Lancelot said. I'm tired of fighting and I'm more interested in studying for my flute exams. Why don't you go back to your throne and I'll go back to my elves. Every year we can meet and tell each other what we have seen.

Very well, said Galahad.

But the next year when he came back, Galahad found only a note. Dear Galahad, it said, I heard there is a nunnery on Mars and I have gone there to join Guenevere. You are too perfect to understand but I hope you will forgive me. Yours truly, Lancelot.

Galahad was the perfect knight and the last knight. He died in the quest for the Holy Grail. The astronauts have searched for Galahad but they will not find him no matter how hard they look.

Someday Galahad will come back to earth to lead a new quest for the Holy Grail. Meanwhile he sits on the moon and amuses himself by throwing Pepsi cans at the Pacific Ocean.

SPADINA TIME

His stomach empty as a broken bottle
He remembers good time garbage: hollowed
Grapefruit halves, coffee grounds and egg
Shells. I can hear you, he says,
Talking to no one at all, seeing himself
Walking down the street, feet against the pavement,
Carrying a wet sheet snapped around a telephone pole
Eating clouds
Watching a herd of city cattle
Being led across an intersection.

I can hear you, he says
His elbows are covered with wax
Talking to the woman in his bed
She is specific to him.
Blue eyes, freckles, a basket of speckled eggs
Compose the morning:
She breathes her goodbye
He memorizes her small breasts
And the way her waist slides into her hips
Her skin covers her completely
With certain exceptions.
He memorizes her small breasts
The angle of her neck
The exact feeling of the feeling of
Sliding into her
The way her waist slides into her hips
The way he always does
With certain exceptions.

His nights stretch before him
A thirty-seven course meal he must
Eat non-stop
Until he collapses.

I can hear you, he says. His elbows are covered with wax, talking to the woman in his bed: she is specific to him. Blue eyes, freckles, a basket of speckled eggs compose the morning. She breathes her goodbye. He memorizes her small breasts and the way her waist slides into her hips, her skin covers her completely with certain exceptions. He memorizes her small breasts, the angle of her neck, the exact feeling of the feeling of sliding into her the way her waist slides into her hips, the way he always does with certain exceptions.

His nights stretch before him, a thirty-seven course meal he must eat non-stop until he collapses. There is a restaurant where he knows the waitress, particularly the backs of her knees and the way her dress fits over her as if she knew. She serves him mounds of rice to which he adds salt, pepper and butter. A fork, saliva and numerous enzymes. A bottle, a loaf of bread and beautiful music. A glance at the waitress in the tiger stripe hair.

Waitress.

Yes.

Pray for me.

She sits down beside him and reads from a Gideon bible. The words flow over him and he feels at peace. That will be fifteen cents, she says.

I want to make my world over.

Then do it, she says. She moves away from the table and encloses herself behind the counter.

He pretends that he will put away what he doesn't like, go to a place without people and set entrance requirements, live outside in the snow. His rice reminds him to pretend that he is in China, to bicycle through the streets of Peking or build a hut in Tibet.

She wore a red coat. Standing beneath a streetlamp in winter covered with illuminated snowflakes she waited for him. He memorized the angle of her neck, the way she was trying to be jaunty and lean against the lamp as if it was a poolroom. She was wearing mittens, it was ridiculous the way the snow had crusted up in the wool, you expected her to be dragging a toboggan. She had a piece of cardboard under her arm; they walked up Spadina to the reservoir, turning around to watch their footprints, pulling each other on the cardboard, tangling themselves up in that one particular time.

Snow down the neck. Running in icicles down his back, he is suddenly inside his clothes. They have given up on the cardboard and are rolling down the hill, the lights of the apartment building, then a blur, then a long sweep of sky and just as the stars become visible they are replaced by a box of yellow balconies. Lying at the bottom everything still moving even with closed eyes he hears her breathing and rolls over to her. She is lying face down in the snow.

How are you, she says, not moving. She says that sometimes after love-making but he wouldn't have thought the same person could roll down a hill in a red coat. Later he sees that one shin is bruised. Her skin is so incredibly translucent, absolutely young and pale.

It's alright, she says, laughing at him, poking him in the stomach. I just bruise easily, that's all. You should have seen me one time when I fell out of a tree. Her breath catches. At first he liked it, thought it was good that they could move to and from each other, but now he hates to lose her. He waits for her to pass through her memories. He feels that when she comes back he will have to start all over, re-establish intimacy, find a place she has never been kissed.

God, you're touchy, she said. He stood at the corner window of his room counting exhaust fumes.

I've forgotten it already, he said sullenly.

But there was no it. She came up behind him. He knew she would wrap her arms around him, sway back and forth with him.

She is specific to him: he knows that in five years he will still have perfect recall of every moment. When he stays at her place they have grapefruit, eggs, fresh percolated coffee. They have a ritual of going outside for a walk first and then coming back and making love. The grapefruit goes off in his stomach like a bomb.

He had a job lining up once every two weeks at the unemployment office. It didn't pay very well but it wasn't demanding. It bothered him to see the older men, wearing thigh-length car coats, standing in line knowing that their bank accounts had disappeared, their mortgages had disappeared, many things had disappeared.

When he first met the girl they were both surprised. It was at night, in a candy store. What am I doing? she said later.

I don't know, he said. What *are* you doing? Their limbs were columned by the light and with her hands she flashed signals on the wall.

That was the first time he was unfaithful to the waitress. He wondered, looking at the backs of her knees, what she would think if she knew. She sat down beside him to watch him eat his rice.

I've got something to tell you, he said. I'm being unfaithful to you with a girl with translucent skin. She wears a red coat and sometimes we walk past here.

Good for you, she said. Did anyone ever tell you that you are irresistible to women?

No.

Good, she said. Why don't you come to dinner sometime?

What will your husband say?

It's better than watching television.

When his landlord rented him the room they stood in the centre of it for a long time assessing each other. No visitors after ten-thirty, said the landlord.

Erik kept in mind that the landlord lived in the adjacent duplex. I have to have visitors after ten-thirty. It's not human to be alone all the time.

But no noise.

No noise.

One day he heard an elephant on the stairs, huffing and groaning with the effort of the climb. He had read that elephants are as graceful as ballet dancers. This elephant was rhythmically smashing its great feet into the wood. It was pushing something ahead of it; he could hear it scraping along the stairs. Perhaps it had injured its trunk. It reached Erik's door. It sighed softly and then collapsed.

Erik opened his door. Crumpled on the landing was the most human being in one place that Erik had ever seen. In front of him was a huge cardboard box filled with underwear and white shirts. He took a card out of his pocket.

If I hand you this card
Call this number.

Hello? somebody handed me this card and it said to call this number.

Harold, the voice said. Is he alright?

Just a moment. Erik ran back up the stairs. Harold was leaning against the wall with his shirt undone. Your mother wants to know if you are alright.

I'm fine, he said. Don't worry about me.

Harold: thirty-two years old, three hundred and eleven pounds, six feet two inches tall, only son of a wealthy widow who owns a shopping plaza, recently run away from home to become a painter, has white shirts, underwear, a broken kettle, a box of watercolours, seventy-two paintings, goes to the Y twice a week to have a sauna, comes up the stairs at ten-thirty every night.

They started to keep track of Harold one night when they were making love. They noticed, woven through their own noises, threatening even to drown them out, the sounds of an elephant in heat. Don't worry, Erik said, it's Harold and he's fine.

Who's Harold?

The elephant who's panting through the keyhole.

The candle is their magic lantern: her hands throw arcane shadows on the wall. Limbs are columned by the light. She has made him come alive without warning. You'll grow, she said, kneading his stomach, but you are tense. She paints him in cowl and cape, moving down a road in twilight. He puts her behind him, walking at a distance with their bowl. She makes herself into an organ grinder and he jumps around a leash.

> *Dear Erik,*
> *Last night I slept with someone else. I am not trying to hurt you by telling you this but I thought we should be open. . .*

You see? he said. I thought I was being faithful to you but actually she was being unfaithful to me.

Yes, I see. Why don't you come home with me?

What will your husband say?

She was only a person disguised as a waitress. Her husband was non-existent. She didn't want to take off her slip.

How can we go to bed if you're wearing that?

It's easy.

We could turn off the lights.

That's not the point.

What is the point?

Maybe I'm hiding something. Do you want to see it?

Yes.

She took off her slip. Now, she said, take off that ridiculous cape. She was altogether different.

Why must you be a romantic? She was lacing up her boots. She had a new scarf. She had accumulated past and future lovers. It was impossible to imagine her in the winter, leaning against a lamp post, wearing mittens crusted with snow. What do you want me to do?

They were striking poses for each other in his room. Right on schedule, as they talked, the elephant lumbered through the front door of the house and started its journey up the stairs. Each time Erik began to speak he was interrupted by the sound of splintering wood. Finally it reached the top landing and stood there, panting at the door. Come in, Erik said. He opened the door. Harold was wearing a grey overcoat, too heavy for spring, and carrying a bag of groceries. Erik gestured towards the room and repeated his invitation.

Harold sat down on the bed beside the girl. His hair, thin tiny blond curls, was plastered against his skull. He pulled three plastic cups of yogurt from his bag and handed them around. Strawberry yogurt, Harold said. It's the best kind.

They ate in silence. When they were finished the girl stood up and put on her coat and gloves. Goodnight, she said to Harold. Erik walked downstairs with her. I guess we won't be seeing each other, he said.

Don't be romantic.

He went back up. Harold was still on the bed; he was eating a second cup of yogurt. Strawberry, Harold said. It's the best kind. When he was finished he put all the empty cups in his bag. He was still wearing his overcoat. Don't worry, Harold said, you must have another girl.

I do, but it's not the same.

Erik had not closed his door so they heard the sound of the key in the lock downstairs, the sound of steps coming up towards them. The waitress paused at the top and looked into Erik's room. Come in, Erik said. She walked over to the bed and sat down beside Harold. Harold put one of his round padded hands on her knee.

How did you know I lived here? Erik asked.

I didn't.

You come round and give bible readings.

No, she said, but I will. She took a bible out of her purse and began reading in a low sonorous voice. That will be free, she said when she was finished.

The girl with the translucent skin came back to visit him. He had memorized her but it wasn't the same. She seemed puffy and distended. She had strained her eyes looking soulfully into the eyes of other men. He thought in terms of her plumbing.

Why must you be a romantic? Her face snapped in and out of focus. Don't you want to be happy? She was spitting grapefruit pits onto her plate.

I'm feeling very glib, she said. They were lying on her bed, the blankets piled between them. I'm feeling very glib, she said, and that's why I don't want to talk. She reached down her throat, took out her voicebox, and put it under the pillow. There, she mouthed, that's better.

The days disappeared suddenly so that he was left, always, with the nights stretching endlessly before him. He went without eating and then he ate until he couldn't move. The waitress read him consolations but the words slurred and dissolved as he heard them. If she was hiding something he couldn't find it.

He remembered a girl who leaned against a streetlamp in winter, wearing mittens, the wool crusted up with snow. He clanked up and down the street in rusty armour, wheeling at the corners, waiting for the spring sun to melt him naked. He walked up to the reservoir one day and discovered, beside it, a ravine running under a bridge. After that he went to the ravine every day to observe the progress of the season. The snow was melting and ran in tiny streams from tree to tree. It ran in small ditches at the bottom of the ravine and in hollow grooves under the remaining snow. He would sit there, his back against a tree, letting the sounds of moving water accumulate until they swallowed the noise of the traffic above. He would pretend he was somewhere else, perhaps bicycling through the streets of Peking or living in a mountain hut in Tibet.

Pieces of soot and twigs absorbed the heat of the sun and dug themselves perfect graves in the snow. But amazingly the leaves and grass, where they showed, were not covered with a layer of black.

Pieces of soot and twigs absorbed the heat of the sun and dug themselves perfect graves in the snow. From his hiding place, through the branches, he could see an apartment building, the same one that had revolved about him as he rolled down the hill in the snow. There was a woman who came out every day and hung a sheet on the railing of her balcony. She did it every day, even when it rained; he wondered if it was a signal to some lover, or perhaps even to him. Sometimes when the weather was good she would stand there and pretend to look for birds with her binoculars. He waved at her but there was no response.

What do you do all day? Harold asked.

I walk around.

There was a girl here to see you.

She wore a sweater and slacks. Standing beneath the streetlamp in early summer she tapped her toes on the pavement and waited for him. He memorized the angle of her neck, the way she laughed with the passerbys and leaned against the lamp post as if it were her house. She was carrying a straw bag and the handles were bound together by a red scarf. They walked up Spadina to the reservoir, turning around to see how far they had come, tangling themselves up in everything that hadn't happened.

How are you? she asked. They were lying on top of the hill, looking down at his ravine.

I'm fine, he said. How are you?

Terrible, she said. It was getting dark and the cars were turning off their headlights. I had a fight with the man I'm living with and I quit my job.

That's too bad, Erik said. But things will work out for the best.

Yes, I know they will.

Tell me about the man you're living with.

It's hard to describe him. But I think you would like him.

We could go out for a beer and get to know each other.

What have you been doing lately?

I sit under the tree over there and meditate on the thin white light of my memory of you.

Don't be so romantic, she said. Back in his room he felt suddenly ridiculous, as if he was stripping for his execution.

Why are you laughing?

Because I don't know why we're doing this.

I don't either. She poked him in the stomach. You'll

learn but you are very slow. Her fingers flashed shadows on the wall. She tried to turn him into a beggar with a cape and cowl but he escaped her and walked down a sunny dirt road, thumbs in the loops of his pants, kicking up dust with his heels.

It was ten-thirty. Right on time Harold began his struggle up the stairs, breathing heavily, testing each step to make sure it would hold his weight. Twice it sounded as if he had died, but each time he revived himself and continued the ascent. He had someone with him. Come on, Harold, she would say, you can make it. When they finally got to the top landing, he paused at the keyhole.

Come in, Erik said.

The four of them sat in a circle in Erik's room. The waitress took out her bible and began to read in the candlelight. Her voice moved through them in the dark, wound around the furniture and the edges of the walls in long intricate patterns. As she read Erik remembered his ravine: the way the bark turned a particular shade of brown with the first spring rains, the woman sending signals from her balcony, the time an impossible wild canary had landed on a branch right beside him, stared at him, and then flown away. The waitress's voice moved through the dark, washed out his thoughts, filled the room with brass church spires and cloudless blue skies. The girl caressed his neck, absently poked among the tangled nerve complexes.

That will be free, the waitress said when she was finished. She stood up and held out her hand to Harold. Come on, she said, we haven't got all night.

Tell me about the man you're living with.

He moved out two weeks ago.

Are you sorry?

No.

What did you talk about?

The weather, she said. He was especially interested in Peruvian weather. He used to keep a chart above the bed.

You must have met him in a drugstore.

Yes, she said. He had terrible itches. She was sitting crosslegged, her elbows resting on her thighs, the tips of her fingers pressed together. What are we going to do?

I don't know, Erik said. He had a job, lining up once every two weeks at the unemployment office. It didn't pay very well but it wasn't demanding. It bothered him to see the older men, wearing their thigh-length car coats, standing in line knowing that their bank accounts had disappeared, their mortgages had disappeared, many things had disappeared.

COLUMBUS AND THE FAT LADY

He moved aimlessly through the fairgrounds, letting the August sun warm him, filter through the dust and fill the gaps in his time. A tall man in his early forties, he wore a vaguely Spanish costume: tight black pants and an embroidered silk shirt. He had a sharp bearded face and large dark eyes. Despite his lack of direction he moved carefully, like a cat sensing its path. Occasionally he stopped and rubbed his hands across his ribs. They had never healed quite properly and he was aware of his body pushing out against them.

"Christopher." Rena, the Fat Lady, waved him towards her. She was sitting out behind her tent, her dress hitched up over her enormous thighs. He went and sat down beside her in a lawnchair. He took off his shirt and stretched himself out to the sun. A scar in the shape of a cross had been burnt into his chest. "Help yourself," she said, meaning the bourbon that was standing in the shadow of her chair. He drank directly from the bottle and then passed it to her. Her face was rippled like a pile of bald pink tires. "Praise the Lord," she said when she had finished. She wiped her mouth and put the bottle back on the ground. They sat and contemplated the taste of the bourbon. Christopher took another drink and passed the bottle to Rena. "Praise the Lord," she said each time she drank. And then, shaking out the last drops, "I know you're not supposed to drink in the sun." She giggled. "Yes," she said, "I surely know you're not supposed to drink in the sun. They say it makes you talk too much. At least it makes me talk too much. It makes me *want* to talk too much. Lord yes." She had a voice that was thin and husky at the same time. "Christopher," she said, "sometimes I believe you myself. Yes I do. But do you believe me?" She looked at him earnestly, across half an empty bottle. He nodded. "Yes," she said, "it's real for sure." She took a handful of her face and shook it. "It's all real. Took me ten years." She traced out the scar on Christopher's chest. "Yes," she said, "I do believe it's real. It must have smelled something awful." Her finger had filled the gouge the iron had left. At first the scar tissue had been bright red but now it was dull and tough. He was tanned from his mornings in the sun. Felipa didn't like to come outside with him. She stayed pale and cool.

He stood up. The bourbon had made him dizzy but not drunk. "It's time," he said. He kissed her hand and put on his shirt.

"Oh," Rena said. "You have such beautiful manners." He kissed her hand again and then started on his way. He had spent months on the ocean but he didn't have thc sailor's rolling gait; he walked like an ocelot sensing its path. He waved at the candy floss man, at the foot-long hot dog booth, at the man who had a new gimmick that was guaranteed to open cans in three seconds, worked his way through the games and gadgets until he came to the midway. The crowds were beginning to fill up the spaces between the tents. Some of the barkers had already started, advertising their three-breasted women, their dwarves and talking animals. He came to his own tent and signalled to a man wearing a striped shirt and a straw hat. He was sitting on the stage with Diego, showing him how to cheat at cards.

"He learns quick," the man shouted to Christopher. Diego pocketed the cards and went to stand beside his father.

"Come on," Christopher said. "We'd better go inside." The man dusted off his pants and ground out his cigar. He cleared his throat. He spat on his hands and rubbed them together. He climbed onto the platform in front of the tent, cleared his throat once more, whistled loudly into the microphone, and began:

> *"Ladies and gentlemen, step right up, yes. . . ."*

On either side of the tent were large crude posters showing a trio of old-fashioned ships tossing in a storm at sea.

> *"Step right up and see the world's most amazing freak of time, right here, ladies and gentlemen, come right in, only twenty-five cents, see Christopher Columbus and*

his ships, hear him tell about his famous voyage, see the man who found America, ladies and gentlemen, the world's strangest freak from time, see the cross they burnt onto his chest, hear about the women he left behind him, the man who met kings and princes, Christopher Columbus, only twenty-five cents, you have to see it to believe, it's absolutely true ladies and gentlemen, bring your children, bring your friends, this is the world's only living history, hear him tell about the Santa Maria. . . ."

Water slopped across the deck of the ship, leaving flecks of foam and seaweed in its wake. Columbus was hunched into his coat, scanning the strange shore and estimating how much longer he could go without sleep. His hand moved in his pocket, seeking the familiar shape of the bottle. Fatigue had permeated him. It was like having a sliver in his nervous system. He uncorked the bottle: it wasn't working for him any more, it might have been thin wine or water. His tongue and throat were so immune it just drained down into the bowl of his stomach.

In his dream he was on land and that, as he came to consciousness, was the first thing he was aware of. "Christopher," the boy was saying, "Christopher." He was making the name into an incantation. He opened his eyes. He was lying in a room lit by a lantern.

"Don't worry," Columbus said. He closed his eyes.

"Don't worry," a woman's voice echoed as he was falling back to sleep. He thought again that they must be on land. He felt the boy's lips on his hand. Tears. The water slid along the polished surface of his skin. They had tied him to a giant wooden wheel and were rolling him slowly through the village. When his cousin had died on the rack he had stayed outside all night watching constellations slip off the edge of the earth. The priest's face was covered with tiny pouches, his eyes grey and certain. He walked along the Spanish coast with Columbus, one night when the clouds were layered into prayers. Columbus knelt down on the grass to confess. He closed his eyes and saw flesh being ground between mill-stones.

"You will feel better," the priest said. "A man does not have to carry his sins."

"Yes," Columbus said. Another cousin had been taken during a storm. He had seen him lose his balance, start sliding across the wet wood. He had dived flat across the deck to save him and had cracked his ribs. Afterwards, still in the rain, they had bandaged him tightly while he drank to distance the pain. He remembered the man's wife. She had long black hair that had crackled in his hands.

"We only ask you to believe," the priest had said, looking pointedly at Columbus, raising the question.

"Yes," Columbus had said. While they bandaged him he kept seeing the widow, crossing herself over an empty grave.

The stone walls were seamed with damp lichen. They had given him a wooden bench to sit on. From the next room he could hear the meshings of clockwork gears mingled with the screams of heretics. But every morning and every evening he knelt and rested his head on the wood. He didn't dare use words any more. He just closed his eyes and held Felipa in his mind. When the image was clear she could move around and whisper to him.

When they brought him in the priest was there, his hands clasped in front of his grey robe. "You will feel better," the priest said. "A man does not have to carry his sins." Columbus nodded. He kissed the priest's bony hands. The skin caught in his teeth and moved around loosely.

With his compasses and sextant he had searched for God on the open sea. When he stumbled on the new world he half expected to find Him, sitting on a great carved throne, unsurprised that He had finally been discovered by mortals. The skin caught in his teeth and moved around loosely. He clamped his jaws; blood vessels popped open like grapes in his mouth.

Felipa caressed him as he slept. She drew her hands across the muscles of his back and plied his spine. Each day the water had been different. He would stand on the deck and try to read its moods, calculate the margin of its mercy.

In his dream he was on land and that, as he came to consciousness, was the first thing he was aware of. Felipa was holding a steaming bowl of soup out to him. He sat up and took the bowl. He smelled it and circled the strange aroma with his tongue. Diego was sitting beside the bed, watching him eat. "You hurt your elbow," Diego said. "It's all swollen up like an egg." Columbus set the soup down and slid his hand along his arm. The lump was big but not painful.

"There's a reporter here to see you," Felipa said. "She said you told her to come today."

Columbus sat up straight. They had a cot for him, backstage, for when he fainted. He could see the sun setting through the yellowed plastic window of his tent. "It's getting better," he said. "This time I was still conscious when I hit the floor."

"No," Felipa said. "It's not good." She frowned. "The doctor said you mustn't do it any more." The reporter had come in and was taking notes.

"I can't help it." He saw the reporter. She had crouched down and was taking his picture.

"I'm going to Rena's," Diego said. "I guess I'll sleep there." He looked sadly at the reporter and his father. "I'll see you tomorrow."

"What made you decide to discover America?"

Columbus lay back on his cot and closed his eyes. "I'm sorry," Felipa said. "He's not very good at giving interviews." She stood between Columbus and the girl. The girl put away her notebook and snapped her camera into its leather case.

"I don't mind," she said. "I just wanted to meet him."

"Maybe some other time. He's very tired." She edged the reporter out of the tent. When she came back in, Columbus was brushing his hair. "Don't worry," she said. "Everything's going to be fine."

He nodded. Lying on the cot, he had suddenly been reminded of rows of men in cells waiting for time to pass. The memory made him uncomfortable. His finger traced the scar on his chest. "Is there time for a drink?"

"Yes there is. But *please,* it won't be bad tonight."

"I know," he said. "If we could just settle somewhere I would get my bearings."

"I'm sure they're going to give you the job. The professor was very interested. He even invited us to dinner."

"I don't mind this," Columbus said.

"It's not healthy. Every time you tell the story, you faint."

That evening they went through the usual interrogations. His heart and pulse were checked. They shone lights into his eyes and poked at his ribs. They had a tape recorder and asked him questions about the Spanish Court.

When they were finished they left Christopher and Felipa in the dining room while they retired to deliberate. Professor Andras was the first to come out. He looked puzzled.

"Well?"

"They won't hire you but they will pay you a small fee to stay on if you will let them question you. You would be welcome to live here but my wife—" he shrugged his shoulders. "I'm sorry, Mr. Columbus."

"It doesn't matter." When they were back in their hotel room they lay on their bed in the dark listening to the breeze breathe through the curtains. He still remembered the man's wife. He had met her only once, by accident, at the edge of the forest.

"I don't want him to go," she had said. Then she had drawn him back into the trees and embraced him. "Forgive me," she had said, "make him stay." The impact of his body had snapped the railing. It had been impossible to hear him above the storm but they had seen him fighting hopelessly in the water.

* * *

"Yes," Felipa said. "This is how it was, before." She gestured broadly, including everything in the sweep of her hand: the redwood trees, the long sandy beach, the Pacific Ocean stretching towards the Orient. Diego was already splashing and swimming in the water but Christopher and Felipa were sitting under a tree by a small stream that fed into the ocean.

"It's very beautiful," Christopher said.

"Yes."

"It seems a strange kind of ocean."

"Maybe we could sell the truck, get a job on a freighter or something."

"No," he said. "I'm tired of the sea." They stood up and walked back to the truck, to get food and their bedrolls. Rena was waiting for them there, talking with a strange girl. The girl had a camera and was taking pictures of them as they came towards her. She had arrived on a motorcycle; it was parked beside the truck. There was a dead snake beneath the rear wheel. She put down her camera and took out her notebook.

"Hello," the girl said. "I followed you."

"What do you want?"

"I want to do something different," she said. "You know, what kind of person you are, how are you with your wife and child. That kind of thing. For example, you could tell me who your favourite pop star is."

"I was born in Genoa in 1450," Columbus said. "When I was nine years old I was apprenticed to a weaver." He hadn't thought about that for a long time, the rhythms of wool and patterns, the miraculous transformation of single strands into shawls and blankets.

"What made you decide to discover America?"

Columbus sat down on the sand beside the truck and closed his eyes. "I'm sorry," Felipa said, "he's not very good at giving interviews."

"I don't mind," the girl said. "I just wanted to meet

him." She put away her notebook and snapped the camera into its leather case. "I took psychology at college. Last week I interviewed a guy who thought he was Jesus Christ."

"Maybe he was."

"Oh yes," the girl said. "I've always believed in reincarnation. My grandmother was Queen Elizabeth the First. I had to curtsy and kiss the hem of her dress every time I came into the room."

Rena had her lawnchairs and her bourbon. She pointed the bottle towards the girl and motioned her to sit down. The girl was wearing tight white shorts, rolled up as far as they would go. "Have a drink," Rena said. She handed the bottle to the girl. The girl unscrewed the cap, wiped the neck of the bottle carefully, and took a delicate sip. She coughed. "Praise the Lord," Rena said. She took a long swallow. "Praise the Lord," she said again and handed the bottle back to the girl. The girl shook her head. "Come on, it won't hurt you." The girl accepted the bottle, took another delicate sip. This time she didn't cough. "Praise the Lord," Rena said. "What's your name?"

"Laura Nimchuk," the girl said.

"I'm pleased to meet you, Laura. That's Christopher Columbus down there and this is his wife, Felipa Moniz de Perestrello. And the boy on the beach is Diego, their son. Praise the Lord." She threw the empty bottle past Laura into the back of the truck. "It took ten years," Rena said. "I never stopped eating. I had to borrow money from the bank. It was a business investment. At the end I got a contract; I had to gain fifty pounds in the last two months and it nearly killed me."

"God," the girl said.

"And it's all real too. Here, feel it."

"I don't know," Columbus said. "I said I was going to India but all along I knew I would discover America. I guess I finally did it because I had to." The girl was stroking Rena's arm. She spread out her fingers and ploughed her hands through the flesh. "It was a very hopeful thing to do. I felt we needed a new beginning." He got up and paced as he talked. "I thought there must be some place untouched by time." The girl was still discovering Rena. It was like exploring a huge geography of lukewarm spaghetti.

"It's real," Rena said. "It's not a fake at all. People used to accuse me of wearing pillows and falsies, all sorts of things. But it's all real. It was hard work too. Don't believe what you hear about glands. I have a picture of myself when I was a girl. I was just as thin as you."

"I believe you," Laura said. "You've really accomplished something." Her hands scooped up loose flesh around a shoulder and shaped it into a vase.

"They didn't want me to go."

"I ate twenty-five apple pies in three days." They had broken him of course. He had written endless pages of confessions, lists of heresies and failures to believe.

"It's not your fault," the priest had said. "Perhaps you are possessed. I've heard of such cases." His face was covered with tiny pouches, his eyes grey and certain. "Especially since your cousin regained his faith at the end. We could try to help you, to purge you of these things."

"Or?"

"A man does not have to carry the burden of his sins," the priest said. "Not in this life." After his confessions they gave him a wooden bench to sit on. Twice a day, in the morning and the evening, Columbus knelt and rested his head on the wood. He didn't dare use words any more. From the next room he could hear the meshings of clockwork gears.

"Jelly rolls, ice cream, chocolates – they're not any good at all. The best you can do with those is get flabby. You need something that will give you a good firm base. People don't understand that. They try to put it all on at once. Bourbon and beer, they're very good for after, pass me my purse, Laura, they feed the flesh, But what you need to begin with are grains and molasses." She giggled. "I know it sounds silly about the molasses but I believe it, it sticks it all together. Feel that: it's quite firm underneath. A person doesn't want to cover themselves with goop. Like you take the lady before me, she was disgusting. Praise the Lord. She was just a slob. People don't pay good money just to see a slob. It's a science really. Without discipline it's almost impossible to get above three hundred pounds. Of course you have to have the talent too. I guess you're just born with it. Praise the Lord. My father taught me everything. He used to be able to put it on any part of his body at will: an arm, or a leg, or even his head. He could never get it on everywhere at once though so he couldn't get steady work. He used to make bets with people. In one week he could double the weight of any part of his body. It's science really, but it's not the kind of thing they teach in school, Lord, I am thirsty, getting dehydrated is the big danger, yes, feel that: it's nice and moist, I make sure to keep it that way, yes."

They had burned the cross into his chest to make sure he would carry his faith to the new world. "A man can protect himself by the sign of God upon his body," the priest had said. He had waited until Columbus regained consciousness and had gently wiped his face with cold water. It was weeks before he could move comfortably. "My own sign is chastity but that is given to very few." He squeezed the cloth over the wound. When Columbus screamed, the priest slapped his face. "We are not trying to punish you. That is what you have to understand."

"If you want my secret in one word, I guess it was porridge."

"I don't think of myself as a hero," Columbus said. He had eaten dinner with the Queen of Spain. When she sent for him the priest smiled, satisfied that he had had his audience first. Laura was sitting on Rena's lap. She had her notebook out again and was taking it all down in shorthand.

"Because of what happened time doesn't exist for me," Columbus said. A tall man in his early forties, he wore a vaguely Spanish costume. He had a sharp bearded face and dark eyes. He was leaning against the truck again. "I don't know why it's real for anyone. There are always gaps, unexplained moments."

"You dream," Laura said. "At night and sometimes during the day you dream."

"I dream about my father," Rena said. "He was always changing his shape. The only part of him that stayed the same was his feet. He could never do anything with his feet. He said it saved him a fortune in shoes."

Columbus got up and went down to the beach. Diego had found some wood and had started a fire beside the stream. Felipa was there too, rinsing off clams and preparing to cook them in a cast iron kettle. Two men had held him when they taped his ribs. He had met the man's wife only once, by accident. She hadn't wanted him to go. He had a knife and helped Felipa by prying open the clams. "Do you dream?"

"No," she said. "I just have pictures. Trees and castles and lakes and things like that. But no one ever talks. In real dreams people talk. Last night I saw a white rabbit."

"Sometimes you have to make a sacrifice," the priest had said. "It might be someone or something very close to you, something that is felt as a great loss. Or it might be something that you aren't even aware of. In such cases it can take years to discover what has been given."

"There must be something constant."

"God's love." The clams hissed as they were plunged into the boiling water. When he had dinner with the Queen he remembered his manners and didn't talk with his mouth full. But she ate carelessly, tearing the fowl apart with her fingers and throwing the remains over her shoulder.

"Yes," Rena said. "I believe everything he says, even the part about the Queen asking him to bring back souvenirs." She was washing her clams down with bourbon and whole wheat bread. The girl still had her notebook but had lost her pen. She was curled up in the firelight, her head on Rena's lap. Rena stroked her hair and played cards with Diego.

"Let's play strip poker," Diego said.

"Lord," Rena laughed. "You're too young. The sight of

me would kill you." Her voice was thin but husky. "But I will if Laura does."

"Are you really his son?" Laura asked later.

"Yes."

"Really?"

"Yes." Her shorts lay on the beach, flashing in the moonlight.

"And you were with him the whole time?"

"The whole time," Diego said. He ran his tongue down the inside of her arm. The moon had laid a superhighway across the ocean.

"What was it like?"

"It was fun. But the food wasn't very good."

"I wish I'd been there." She went to the ocean and dipped her foot in the water. She stood ankle deep, looking at herself. Diego came and stood beside her. He put his arm around her. "I don't really wish I'd been there," she said. "I can hardly stand up."

"You get seasick easy?"

"I never have before."

There was noise near the fire behind them. Rena came running and tripping towards them, a blanket wrapped around her, her flesh bouncing out in all directions. "Beware the Spanish Infidels," she was shouting, "beware the Latin Lechers." She rushed up to them and dropped on her knees in front of them. "Save me, Diego," Rena cried. "Save me, I beg of you." She kissed his feet suppliantly. "Save me from your father and anything I have is yours."

"You know I can't interfere," Diego said. "I'm sorry."

"Laura, you'll help me? Please?"

"Of course I will," Laura said. She began leading Rena back towards the fire. "What happened?"

"It's too horrible."

"Now, now," Laura said. "I'll protect you." She waved goodbye to Diego, the ocean, her tight white shorts, the highway to the Orient.

"Goodnight, Laura," Diego said.

"Goodnight, Diego," Rena called. "Keep your eyes on the top card."

Diego walked along the shore until he found Columbus. He was sitting on the beach, drawing maps with a stick. Diego squatted down beside him. The maps showed a clear route from Spain to India. "This is the way it should have been," Columbus said. "All the rest was a mistake."

"Yes."

"Who won your card game?"

"Rena."

* * *

He moved aimlessly through the fairgrounds, letting the sun warm him, filter through the dust and fill the gaps in his time. He had a sharp bearded face; his skin was burnished from the summer. Felipa was not with him. She stayed indoors, pale and cool, preparing for winter.

"Christopher." Rena, the Fat Lady, waved him towards her. She was sitting out behind her tent. He went and sat down beside her in the lawnchair that was beside her own, that she had placed there for him. He took off his shirt and stretched himself out to the sun. A scar in the shape of a cross had been burnt into his chest. "Help yourself," she said, meaning the bourbon that was standing between their chairs. He drank directly from the bottle and then passed it to her. "Praise the Lord," she said after she drank. She wiped her mouth and put the bottle back on the ground.

"It's warm again," he said.

"Indian summer. You could have been the first man to see an Indian." She laughed. "The first white man I mean. It surely would have been something." She laughed again. Her face rippled like a pile of pink tires. "I guess you missed your chance."

There was a taste in his mouth that he'd never noticed before. He didn't know where it had come from. "I guess I did."

"Yes," Rena said. "You surely did pick a strange time

to discover America." She tipped her bottle up high. "Praise the Lord." Laura came out of the tent. She was wearing a dressing gown and carrying a cup of coffee. She rubbed her eyes and blinked.

"Diego's just getting up too," she said. The priest used to like to bring him in supper and watch him eat. He would sit beside him on the bench and watch him as he searched the soup for hidden messages. Diego was ready; he stood at the door of the tent waiting.

"It's time," Columbus said. He kissed Rena's hand. Then he and Diego set out together, walking around so they could come across the midway from the inside, as if by accident. The barker was waiting for them. He wore a striped shirt and a straw hat. They stood beside him for a moment, conferring about details that had been decided a hundred times, and then went inside, ready to begin.

"Its absolutely true, see the world's strangest freak from time, he's right here, yes, ladies and gentlemen, step right up here, it's absolutely true, see Christopher Columbus and his ships, hear him tell about his famous voyage, see the man who found America, ladies and gentlemen, the world's strangest freak from time, see the cross they burnt onto his chest, hear about the women he left behind him, the man who met kings and princes, yes, Christopher Columbus and it's only twenty-five cents, you have to see it to believe it, it's absolutely true, ladies and gentlemen, bring your children, this is the world's only living history, hear him tell about the Santa Maria. . . ."

"Yes," Columbus said, "it's absolutely true." He stood on the stage in his tight black pants and embroidered silk shirt. He winked at the ladies in the audience. When the tent was jammed full the lights would go down. Felipa would come on stage, clicking castanets and singing a throaty Spanish ballad. While Columbus traced lines on the map and told his story she remained onstage, sitting on a velvet cushion. "We had sighted the coast. I had been standing on the bridge of the ship for three days, hoping for land. It hadn't rained for a week. Suddenly a great storm came up. The winds blew the ship around like a matchstick—" he gestured expansively with his hands. His voice was beginning to tremble. "And then, there was a flashing light, a clap—" His arms outstretched, his mouth open, he suddenly stopped. There was a sound like an aborted cough. His arms dropped to his sides. He fell over, unconscious. Felipa knelt beside him. She pulled a scented hankerchief from her bodice and gently stroked his head.

"And then," she said, "he was rescued. He and his son Diego. They were brought to my house in the middle of the night. The ship was utterly destroyed and there were no other survivors." She signalled Diego. They dragged Columbus's body off into the wings. "And now," she said, "I will sing one more song, it is the lament of a widow who has lost her husband at sea."

House of Anansi Fiction (in print)

Five Legs, *Graeme Gibson*
Korsoniloff, *Matt Cohen*
The Telephone Pole, *Russell Marois*
Eating Out, *John Sandman*
A Perte de Temps, *Pierre Gravel*
The String Box, *Rachel Wyatt*
La Guerre, Yes Sir!, *Roch Carrier*
Victor Victim, *Michael Charters*
The Afterpeople, *George Payerle*
The Circuit, *Lawrence Garber*
The Honeyman Festival, *Marian Engel*
Floralie, Where Are You?, *Roch Carrier*
Bartleby, *Chris Scott*
Billy the Kid, *Michael Ondaatje*
When He Was Free And Young And He Used To Wear Silks, *Austin Clarke*
Cape Breton Is The Thought Control Centre Of Canada, *Ray Smith*
Communion, *Graeme Gibson*
Tales From The Uncertain Country, *Jacques Ferron*
Is It The Sun, Philibert?, *Roch Carrier*
The Truth And Other Stories, *Terrence Heath*
No Pain Like This Body, *Harold Sonny Ladoo*

House of Anansi Poetry (in print)

The Dream Animal, *Charles Wright*
The Circle Game, *Margaret Atwood*
Airplane Dreams: Composition from Journals, *Allen Ginsberg*
The Army Does Not Go Away, *David Knight*
Year of the Quiet Sun, *Ian Young*
The Gangs of Kosmos, *George Bowering*
Nobody Owns th Earth, *bill bissett*
Body, *Robert Flanagan*
The Collected Works of Billy the Kid, *Michael Ondaatje*
Soundings, *edited by Jack Ludwig and Andy Wainwright*
Power Politics, *Margaret Atwood*
Mindscapes, *edited by Ann Wall*
Civil Elegies, *Dennis Lee*
Incisions, *Robert Flanagan*